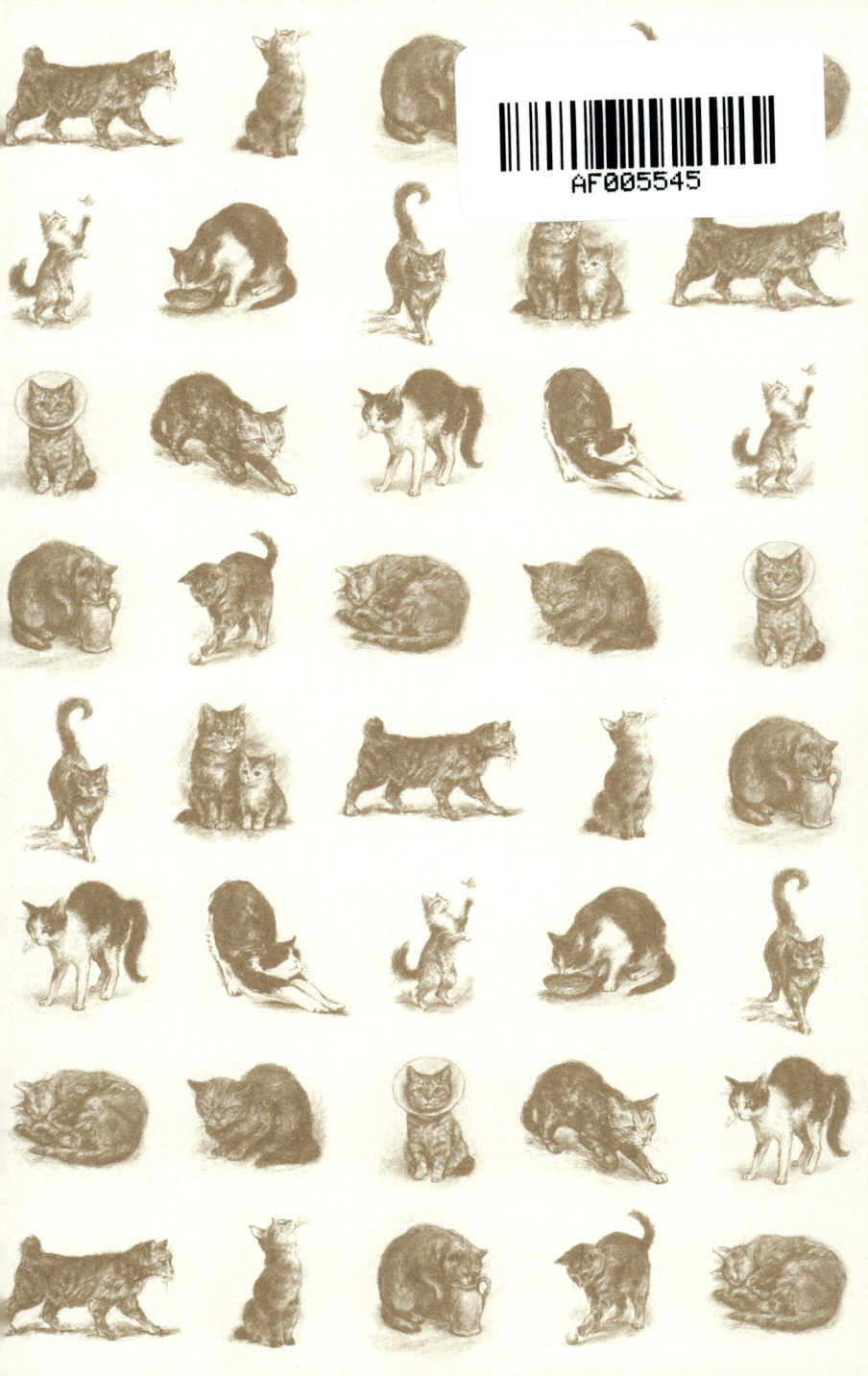

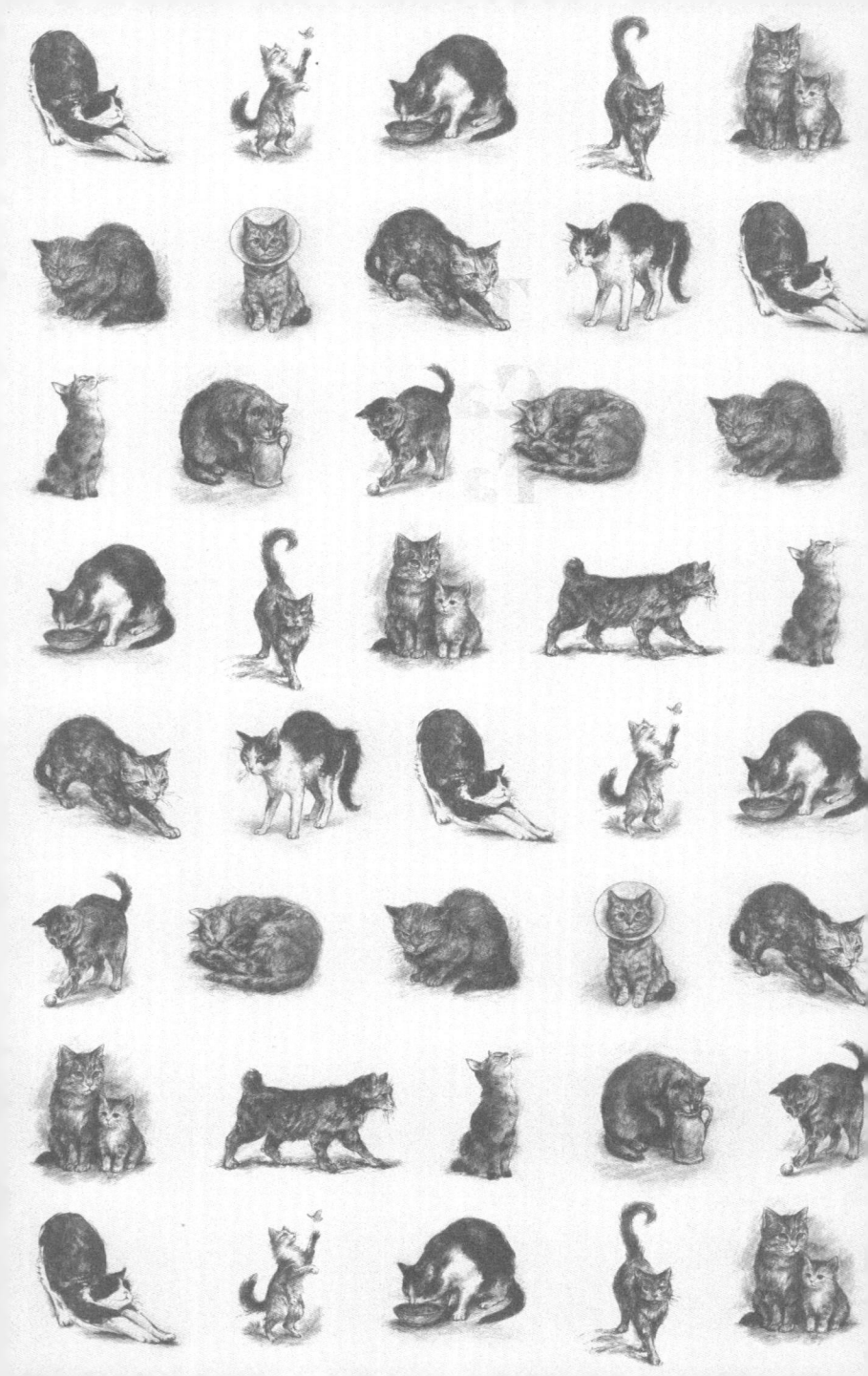

The Cat's Tales

The Cat's Tales

*Feline fairy tales
and folklore*

Charlie Creed

Elliott&Thompson

First published 2025 by
Elliott and Thompson Limited
2 John Street
London WC1N 2ES
www.eandtbooks.com

Represented by:
Authorised Rep Compliance Ltd
Ground Floor, 71 Lower Baggot Street
Dublin, D02 P593
Ireland
www.arccompliance.com

ISBN: 978-1-78396-921-0

Copyright © Charlie Creed 2025

The Author has asserted his right under the Copyright, Designs and Patents Act, 1988, to be identified as Author of this Work.

All rights reserved. No part of this publication may be reproduced, stored in or introduced into a retrieval system, or transmitted, in any form, or by any means (electronic, mechanical, photocopying, recording or otherwise) without the prior written permission of the publisher. Any person who does any unauthorised act in relation to this publication may be liable to criminal prosecution and civil claims for damages.

Illustrations by Tim Oakenfull

9 8 7 6 5 4 3

A catalogue record for this book is available from the British Library.

Typesetting: Marie Doherty
Printed by CPI Group (UK) Ltd, Croydon, CR0 4YY

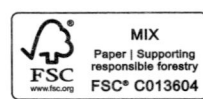

*For Wolfie,
the true King of the Cats*

Contents

Introduction ix

1 How the Cat Came to Be 1
When the Cat Ruled the World · *Chinese* 6
The Cat Who Came Indoors · *Zimbabwean* 9
The Cat's Purr · *Caribbean* 13
Why Cats Always Wash after Eating · *Belgian* 21
Why the Dog Hates the Cat · *Chinese* 25
How the Manx Cat Lost Its Tail · *Manx* 32
Why the Cat Kills Rats · *Nigerian* 36

2 The Mysterious Cat 39
The Little White Cat · *Irish* 44
The Colony of Cats · *Italian* 54
The White Cat · *French* 61
The Bank Cat · *Australian* 69
Johnny Reed's Cat · *English* 77
Kisa the Cat · *Icelandic* 80
The Poor Miller's Boy and the Cat · *German* 88
The Boy Who Drew Cats · *Japanese* 94
The Enchanted Cat · *Hungarian* 99

3 The Mischievous Cat 105
Puss in Boots · *European* 109
Cat and Mouse in Partnership · *German* 115
The Cat and the Birds · *Classical* 120

The Clever Cat · *Berber*	122
The Cat and the Mice · *Tibetan*	132
The Fox and the Cat · *Classical/German*	137

4 The Companion Cat — **139**

Dick Whittington and His Cat · *English*	143
The Cottager and His Cat · *Icelandic*	150
The Cat's Elopement · *Japanese*	154
Venus and the Cat · *Classical*	159
Silvershod · *Russian*	162

5 The Greedy Cat — **167**

The Greedy Cat · *Scandinavian*	171
Catafay and the Fox · *Russian*	175
The Cat and the Cock · *Classical*	181
The Black Cat · *Jewish*	185

6 The Malevolent Cat — **187**

King Arthur and the Cat · *Welsh*	192
The Demon Cat · *Irish*	199
The Cat Witches · *Welsh*	202
The Cat-Witch · *North American*	206
The Nunda, Eater of People · *Swahili*	210

7 The Unfortunate Cat — **217**

The Two Cats · *Arabic*	221
The Story of a Cat, a Mouse, a Lizard and an Owl · *Indian*	225
The Lion and the Cat · *Native American*	229
The Cat and the Crow · *Arabic*	235

Sources	239

Introduction

To many, a home without a cat is a home without a heart. Jean Cocteau called cats a home's 'visible soul'. Delightful, adorable and completely fascinating, they offer us so much. We love them, we care for them, we laugh at them. We feed, indulge and cuddle them. They provide a friend for the lonely and a comfort for the troubled. They are our playmates, our confidants, our friends and our children. They are, quite simply, the most wonderful, most ridiculous creatures in the world: majestic and mysterious, silly and serious, elegant, clumsy, aloof and loving.

Little wonder, then, that the cat's popularity, like its population, has spread across the globe. It has been estimated that between 600 million and a billion cats walk the Earth. The majority live in Asia, home to approximately two-thirds of the world's cats, with China housing the single largest population, at around 70 million pet cats and 50 million strays. A similar number of house cats live in the USA, where one third of all homes boasts a cat. In the pet-loving UK, meanwhile, there are between 10 and 12 million pet cats.

This love affair between humans and cats has endured for millennia. Inevitably, cats feature prominently in our folklore and fairy tales. From England to Japan, North America to Nigeria, humans have told stories about cats. These stories, and their feline stars, display an extraordinary variety: there are plucky cats and lucky cats, good cats and evil cats, crafty, foolish, greedy and fierce cats. They appear as princesses and witches, kings and demons, magical helpers and bloodthirsty monsters.

It is hard to imagine any other animal playing so many roles. After all, animals in fairy tales are often reduced to stock characters, representing one particular quality or type. When readers encounter a wolf in a traditional tale, they know it to be dangerous. Foxes, meanwhile, are sly; owls are wise; monkeys clever; sharks predatory. They are not animals, as such; they are tools storytellers use to spin tales, to satirise, to offer psychological insights. As the French anthropologist Claude Lévi-Strauss said, animals are *'bons à penser'* – that is, good to think with.

Cats, however, have refused to be put in a box (ironically, given their love of them). Cats are simply too elusive, too complex to be so easily explained. And so we find them playing a range of roles in our cultures and our mythologies, often simultaneously and often contradictorily. They have been worshipped as gods, feared as demons, respected as hunters, and loved as companions. They have been symbols of fertility and femininity, domesticity and the home. They have represented hunting and the wild, chaos and violence. They have been linked with the moon and with magic. They have been totems of good fortune and omens of death.

The many-sided nature of cats will be familiar to any cat owner. You never quite know where you are with a cat – even your

Introduction

own. They are the most elegant of creatures, and yet comically clumsy; wise yet foolish, dignified yet farcical, gentle yet fierce. One moment, they are snoring at the end of the bed, the next zooming up a tree. You may watch your cat prowling, stately and superior, or find it wedged between the banister posts. Some days, they are your most affectionate friend, the next, insultingly aloof. They disappear for hours, only to reappear beneath your feet or in the shadows on the stairs.

And who knows what mischief they make in those long, secretive hours when out of sight? Are they sleeping? Chasing mice? Squabbling with their rivals? Possibly. But it would be little surprise to discover they have been casting spells, outwitting foes or ruling kingdoms.

Nevertheless, despite the array of characters assumed by cats in folklore, when the stories are placed alongside each other, certain types emerge. All cultures, it seems, have acknowledged the cat's supernatural side; all have recognised its cunning; all glimpsed a darkness within. And other characteristics – their greed, their lovability – are simply undeniable, inherent to the cat itself. In this book, therefore, after starting off with a chapter on the origins of cats, the stories have been grouped together into six different categories to capture some of their essential elements: the Mysterious Cat, the Mischievous Cat, the Companion Cat, the Greedy Cat, the Malevolent Cat, and the Unfortunate Cat. Consequently, despite the fantastical scenarios in these tales, it is likely the reader will recognise aspects of the cats they know. After all, whose cat isn't a monstrous glutton? Which moggy isn't capable of mischief? Doesn't every old tom, however lazy, harbour a ferocious inner beast?

Such is their universal appeal, cats have featured in hundreds of compelling stories. Here, these have been winnowed down to forty tales from twenty-eight different countries or cultures, with almost all the regions of the world represented. The earliest tales date back thousands of years; the most recent are from the nineteenth century. They are drawn not from literature, nor generally from mythology, but from fairy tales and folklore – that is, from traditional tales, often with oral roots, obscure origins and multiple versions. These stories, lovingly collected, have been retold, trying always to retain a flavour of the original source.

So, whether your cat is a lazy old moggy or a tiny tiger, a sneaky trickster or a supernatural being, it is hoped that you will recognise something of your pet in the following stories. Above all, though, it is hoped that you will enjoy exploring the cat's tales – as endearing, as comical, as mysterious and as peculiar as the cat itself.

1

How the Cat Came to Be

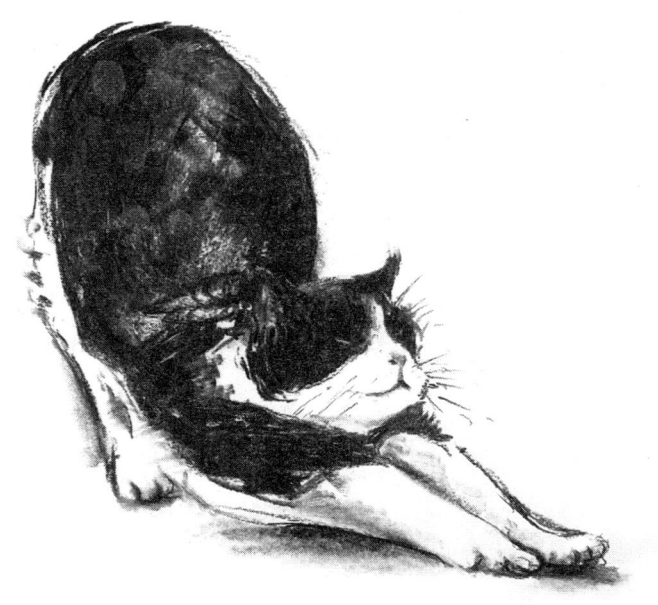

Once there was a great hero named Rustam. The grandson of the king, he was a fearsome warrior, the champion of champions, and his deeds were told throughout the land.

One night, Rustam was returning from a battle when he came upon a band of thieves. They had surrounded an old man, who huddled in fear upon the ground. Rustam, with a few swings of his sword, sent the bandits packing.

As they sat around the campfire afterwards, beneath the night sky, the man – a magician – offered to reward Rustam. But Rustam insisted that he had all he needed. What, he wondered, could be more beautiful than the fire, the smoke and the stars?

At that, the magician stretched out his hand and, to Rustam's amazement, he plucked two shining stars from the sky. Then he picked a flicker of flame from the fire. Finally, he grasped a coil of grey, twisting smoke from the air. Cupping the star, the flame and the smoke in his palms, the wizard began to murmur and mumble – unearthly rhymes and incantations, too quiet for Rustam to decipher. While he spoke, his hands seemed to knead the elements together, working them as though they were lumps of clay.

Finally, after several minutes, the wizard blew into his cupped hands. When he unclasped them, the two shining stars, the flicker of flame and the coil of grey, twisting smoke had vanished. In their place sat a tiny animal. The creature stretched and yawned, its front legs extended before it, a long sinuous tail waving in the air. Rustam saw that its grey fur was the colour of smoke, its tongue flickered like a flame and its eyes sparkled like the stars.

The wizard handed the animal to Rustam, who took it gingerly. It was so small and so fragile – and yet so full of life. The creature rubbed its cheek against the hero's and let out a soft mewl. Then, climbing onto his shoulder, it began to pick determinedly at the man's sleeve, first with one paw, then the other, alternating. Soon the sleeve was dotted with tiny holes.

The hero chuckled with delight. He saw, now, that he had been wrong: there *was* something more beautiful than the fire, the smoke and the stars.

It was a kitten – the first in all the world.

And that was how the cat came to be.

This ancient Persian myth is just one of many stories addressing the origins of cats and how they came to play such important roles in our lives.

The Hopi, a Native American tribe, for example, recount how cats first befriended people. A boy tracked an animal's prints through the snow to a large rock. Peering beneath, he saw a strange creature, small and furry. Taking it home, he fed and cared for it. Soon, he and the creature loved each other dearly – so dearly that the creature never left. After that, the cat and the Hopi remained the firmest of friends.

In a legend common to both Jewish and Islamic cultures, Noah was infuriated by the number of mice on his ark. They simply would not stop multiplying. In despair, Noah asked God for help in getting rid of the mice. In answer, God commanded him to run his hand down the lion's head and back. Noah, of course, did as he was instructed. The moment he did so, the lion let out a great sneeze, long and loud – and a pair of cats flew from its nose.

Now, that was probably *not* how the first cat was created. But, in fact, no one knows exactly when or where cats came to be a part of our lives. One theory maintains that cats became domesticated some 4,000 years ago in Lower Egypt's Nile Delta region. Others believe it began 10,000 or so years ago in the Middle East's Fertile Crescent.

Wherever it took place, it was thanks to the cat's skill at hunting rodents. As people turned away from nomadism to take up agriculture, they found themselves with stores of grain, which, in turn, attracted rats and mice. Delighted to find their prey congregating in one convenient place, wildcats moved in. These African wildcats (or *Felis lybica*) were members of the *Felidae* family, the order of mammals that includes all cats, from lions to the tiny rusty-spotted cat. The earliest *Felid* appeared 25–30 million years ago, with wildcats emerging some 1 or 2 million years ago.

Now, though, these wildcats were making themselves comfortable in human communities. Between the supply of rodents and the people's food waste, they had little reason to leave. Gradually, they ceased being wild and evolved into the domestic cat (*Felis catus*). It suited everyone (except the rodents) perfectly. The humans benefited from the rodent population being controlled, as that protected food supplies and limited the spread of disease, and the cats gained shelter and easy meals.

Ever since then, cats have shared our homes. We have also, somewhat futilely, attempted to *understand* them. As humans always do when we wish to make sense of something, we have woven stories around these cats: tales told round desert fires, and in castle halls, and in tumbledown cottages; stories written on parchment, scribbled on scrolls, printed in books – all to understand *why* cats are as they are.

Such narratives are known as *pourquoi* stories (from the French for 'why') – fictional tales explaining the origin of something. The tales in this chapter are just a handful of the many *pourquoi* stories concerning cats. They attempt to answer such questions as: Why do cats purr? Why do cats live with humans? Why do they hate rats? And loathe dogs?

The stories are delightful and ingenious but they struggle to bring us much closer to answering how the cat came to be. After all, we could never truly understand cats: they are too enigmatic, too inscrutable. However closely we share our lives with them, they will always keep themselves a little separate, a little *other*, with two paws in our world, and two in a world of mystery. But then, what else would you expect from a creature made from a flicker of fire, a coil of smoke and two bright sparkling stars?

When the Cat Ruled the World

· Chinese ·

Chinese mythology tells of a time, shortly after the Earth's creation, when cats were in charge. The experiment did not last long – cats, evidently, don't have the temperament for ruling. They were, however, left with the gift of purring and with an inflated sense of self-importance.

Some versions of the story name the cat in charge as Li Shou. A cat deity, she was considered a protector of families and a symbol of motherhood. She was particularly popular with farmers, for she was believed to bless the harvest – a nod, perhaps, to the role cats play in protecting crops from pests.

A piece of oral folklore, rather than an established fairy tale, the story's origins are murky and disputed.

In the beginning, cats ruled the world.

The gods, having made the Heavens and the Earth, placed the cat in charge. The animal was intelligent, they knew, and would do an excellent job. Accordingly, they bestowed upon it the power of speech, and let it get on with things. The cat, however, soon grew bored. Running the world was rather too much like hard work; it was easier to doze in a patch of sunlight or to chase after leaves in the breeze.

Angered by the cat's idleness, the gods came down to Earth to complain. They found the cat asleep beneath a cherry tree.

'This just isn't good enough,' they said. 'We've given you an important job, and this is how you repay us? All you do is sleep and eat and laze about!'

The cat half opened an eye. 'Well, I didn't ask to be in charge, did I?' it said, stifling a yawn.

'That doesn't matter,' said the gods. 'You have *responsibilities*. Now, go and do your job.'

But the moment the gods departed, the cat closed its eyes and fell asleep once more. It spent the following days chasing mice and resting. 'The world can rule itself,' it thought. 'Why should I bustle about, when I could eat and sleep and ruminate?'

However, without anyone to watch over it, the world descended into chaos.

The gods soon returned.

'I thought we told you to take care of things?' they grumbled. 'Planets don't just run themselves, you know.'

The cat, leg cocked in the air, paused its grooming. 'I'm sorry? Did you say something? I wasn't listening.'

'Right! This is your last chance!' thundered the gods. 'Run the world *properly*, or we'll give the job to someone else.'

'Fine by me,' shrugged the cat. 'To be honest, I'm not that fussed about running the world. It seems rather a dreary business – too much rushing about, giving orders and making decisions. Not really my style. Why don't you pick someone else to govern? The monkeys, perhaps? Or humans? They look like they might enjoy it.'

The gods agreed, accepting that the current state of affairs simply wasn't working. They appointed the humans as the new rulers of the world.

As it turned out, this new arrangement suited everyone: humans could do the chores and feel important, and cats could concentrate on the essential things, like snoozing and snacking.

Now that the cat was no longer the ruler, the gods removed its ability to speak and gave this power to the humans instead. They did, however, allow the cat to retain its purr; for the purr's gentle rumble is the noise the Earth makes as it circles the Heavens. Should the cat ever stop its purring, all that we know would vanish in the blink of an eye. Gone would be the passage of time, the world and the stars above, even life itself.

And that is why the cat always looks so pleased with itself: it never forgets how important it is, or that the gods first chose the cat, not the human, to rule the world.

The Cat Who Came Indoors

· Zimbabwean ·

This story was originally told in Karanga, one of the languages of Zimbabwe's Shona people. Though first published in the 1960s, it is based on a traditional oral tale of unknown age. It offers an account of how the cat first made the transition from a wild creature, surviving in the great outdoors, to our trusted and treasured companion. In this story, though, cats don't simply befriend humans – they specifically befriend women.

Throughout history, cats have been associated with women: from Ancient Egyptian cat goddesses to Diana, Hecate and Venus; from their unfortunate link with witches, to their relationship with the moon, traditionally considered feminine.

Meanwhile, though 'The Cat Who Came Indoors' is a delightful story, it does raise an uncomfortable question: since cats are always on the lookout for a better offer, would they ditch us if one came along?

A cat lived all alone in the jungle. Day after day, she ate and she slept, she slept and she ate. It was a slow, solitary life and, week by week, she grew lonelier and lonelier. She decided to find herself a husband.

'Life's more fun when you share it with somebody,' she said to herself. 'But I can't marry just anyone. My husband must be the finest creature in all the land!'

One day, as she sat on a branch feeling lonely, she spotted another cat wandering through the trees below. He was a handsome tomcat, fat and healthy.

'My word!' she thought. 'What a remarkable individual! He's a fine creature – the finest in all the land!'

So, the cat hopped down from the branch and went to live with the tomcat. And, for a time, they were very happy.

But a few weeks later, the cat and her husband were out and about when there came a rustling sound from the grass ahead. Suddenly, a blur of fur burst from the long grass. It was a leopard! He barged into the little tomcat and sent him flying.

'Oh me, oh my!' thought the cat. 'My husband's not the most remarkable individual after all! No, this leopard is truly a fine creature – the finest in all the land!'

So, the cat left her husband and went to live with the leopard instead. And, for a time, they were very happy.

But, a few weeks later, the cat and the leopard were out and about when they heard a loud growl from behind a tree. Suddenly, a shape whooshed from the bush. It was a lion! It pounced upon the leopard and, scratching and snarling, soon sent him packing.

'Goodness gracious!' thought the cat. 'The leopard's not the most remarkable individual after all! No, this lion is truly a fine creature – the finest in all the land!'

So, the cat left the leopard and went to live with the lion instead. And, for a time, they were very happy.

But, a few weeks later, the cat and the lion were out and

about when they heard the *thump-thump-thump* of footsteps. Suddenly, a giant charged from the trees. It was an elephant! It stomped and stamped until the lion was flat as a leaf.

'Oh dear!' thought the cat. 'The lion's not the most remarkable individual after all! No, this elephant is truly a fine creature – the finest in all the land!'

So, the cat left the lion and went to live with the elephant instead. And, for a time, they were very happy.

But, a few weeks later, the cat and the elephant were out and about when they heard a deafening crack. A figure stepped from the shadows. It was a man with a gun! With a flurry of bangs, the man fired shot after shot at the elephant.

'Gosh!' thought the cat. 'The elephant's not the most remarkable individual after all! No, this man is truly a fine creature – the finest in all the land!'

So, the cat left the elephant and went to live with the man instead. And, for a time, they were very happy. The cat slept on the roof of the man's small house. The thatch was cosy, mice were plentiful and the cat was pleased with her lot.

But, a few weeks later, as the cat dozed on the warm thatched roof, she heard a tremendous din. The man and his wife were arguing. The man shouted at his wife, the woman shouted at her husband, and they both shouted at each other. This went on for quite some time.

Finally, the man tumbled backwards out of the door, followed shortly after by his bags. He slunk off, looking very sorry for himself. 'And don't come back!' shouted the woman.

'Well, I never!' thought the cat. 'The man's not the most remarkable individual after all! No, this woman is truly a fine creature – the finest in all the land!'

So, the cat left the man and went to live with the woman instead. She jumped down from the roof and sauntered into the house. Purring, she curled up on a cushion by the fire and fell asleep.

And, for a time, the cat and the woman were very happy.

In fact, they still are.

The Cat's Purr

· Caribbean ·

Is there a more beautiful sound in the world than a cat purring? A soft velvety roll, bubbling away, soothing and comforting. We generally suppose a purring cat to be a happy cat. However, while it can indicate contentment, cats purr for other reasons too. They may purr in greeting, or to attract attention, or when anxious or unwell.

Given that purring is such a distinctive feature of cats, it is no surprise to find multiple stories addressing its origin. In the British fairy tale 'How Cats Got Their Purr', for example, three white cats save a prince and a princess from a witch's curse by spinning 10,000 skeins of pure white linen thread. As a reward, they are given the gift of purring. Now, in memory of their achievement, cats whirr and hum like a spinning wheel.

The following explanation for the purr's genesis is a Caribbean folk tale, originating from the island of Montserrat. It is, in fact, two pourquoi *stories in one, for it also suggests why the cat and the rat came to be enemies.*

There was once a cat who was best of friends with a rat. No, really. The truth was, Rat looked up to Cat and liked to copy him whenever he could. When Cat learned the flute, Rat learned to play. When Cat built a hut, Rat built one alongside it. When Cat wove a mat, or hung a hammock, or wore a hat, Rat did all those things too. And when Cat found a patch of land and took up farming, Rat started farming the next-door patch. Each morning, they would stroll arm in arm to their land and spend the days working the fields, side by side.

They would sow and hoe, dig and plant. They would plough and pick, water and weed. It was hard, hot work, but through it all they would keep each other company, laughing and joking. Best of all, they would plan the wonderful feast that awaited them when their crops were ready.

'What a meal we'll have when our food is grown!' laughed Cat.

'It will be wonderful!' cried Rat. 'The greatest feast ever known!'

'We'll have papaya and plantains!'

'Guava and mangoes!'

'Soups and barbecues and sandwiches and stews!'

Sometimes, the irrepressible Rat would grow so excited that he'd break into song while they worked:

> My Cat, my Cat, my lovely Cat –
> We'll eat so much that we'll grow fat!
> My Cat, my Cat, my lovely Cat –
> Yes, we are friends, and that is that!

One evening, Cat had a visit from his uncle.

'Nephew, here's a present for you,' the old uncle said. 'Take care of it, for it's been passed down in the family for generations.' And he took a tiny drum from his bag.

'It's beautiful,' said Cat. 'What is it?'

'It's a cat drum,' explained the old uncle. 'Now, be careful when you play it. You must never, ever play it roughly. You must stroke it oh so gently, like this.'

And oh so gently the old uncle stroked the tiny drum.

Puurr-um puurr-um went the drum.

'Now you have a go,' said the uncle.

Cat took the instrument and, as he had been shown, stroked it gently with his paw.

Puurr-um puurr-um went the drum.

'Perfect,' said the uncle. 'Remember though, this is no ordinary drum – it's a cat drum. You must never hit or thump it. And you must never let anyone else play it.'

The following morning, Rat heard an intriguing sound from inside Cat's hut.

Puurr-um puurr-um went the drum.

'Wow, what a noise!' he said, as he rushed inside. 'What music!'

He began to dance around the little hut, singing and clapping.

Puurr-um puurr-um went the drum.

'Hey Cat, can I have a turn?' Rat cried excitedly.

'No, no, Rat,' said Cat. 'Sorry, but this is a cat drum. No one else is to play it.'

'But we do everything together! We always share!' said Rat.

'Sorry, Rat, no can do,' said Cat. 'I promised my uncle: the cat drum is just for me.'

'Not fair!' moaned Rat. 'I want a turn. Give me a go!'

But Cat could not be budged. Rat was upset. Cat had never refused him anything before, and he didn't like it one bit. One way or another, he was going to get his paws on that drum. He needed time to think of a plan.

'Ah! I just remembered!' he said. 'I forgot to have breakfast this morning. Cat, can I have some food, please?'

Cat sighed. 'If you must,' he said, fetching his friend a bowl of porridge. 'But don't take too long. It's time for work!'

Rat ate and he ate, trying to muster up a plan. He ate until his bowl was empty.

'Come on, Rat,' said Cat. 'Stop dawdling; we've work to do in the fields.'

'But I'm hungry,' said Rat. 'I can't work until I've finished. Can I have some more?'

So Cat fetched him a second bowl.

But still Rat ate and he ate, racking his brain for a plan.

'Hurry up, Rat,' said Cat. 'That's enough food, surely?'

'No, no,' said Rat. 'I'm starving. Can I have some more please?'

So Cat fetched him a third bowl.

And, once again, Rat ate and he ate, waiting for an idea to pop into his head.

'Stop now! Please!' cried Cat. 'If you eat any more, you'll make yourself poorly!'

'Ha!' thought Rat. *'There's* my plan! I'll pretend to be ill!'

And he began to groan and grimace, his paws on his belly.

'What's wrong?' asked Cat. 'Are you hurt?'

'Oh! Ah! Ouch!' moaned Rat. 'It's my belly! It aches!'

'Tut! I knew this would happen,' sighed Cat, shaking his head. 'Why were you bolting your food like that, you greedy creature?'

'Oh! Ah! Ouch!' cried Rat. 'It's getting worse!'

'You'd best lie down,' said Cat. And he helped Rat into his bed. 'Now, I have to go to work,' Cat went on, 'but you rest here until you feel better. I'll check on you later.'

'Thanks, Cat,' murmured Rat, weakly. 'You're the best.'

Cat tucked up Rat all nice and snug in bed, then went off to work. The second he was out of sight, however, Rat leapt to his feet.

'Ha! My plan worked perfectly!' he laughed. 'Now I can play the drum!'

Rat grabbed the drum and, hugging it tight, began to play. But he did not stroke it oh so gently. No, he struck it with all his might. He hit and thumped and pounded. He bished and bashed and boshed.

Far away in the field, Cat heard the racket.

'That sounds like someone playing my drum!' he cried, and he ran back to his house.

Rat, however, saw him coming through the window. So, when Cat rushed through the door, the drum was on the floor where he had left it, and Rat was tucked up in bed.

'Hey, Rat, wake up!' Cat cried. 'Was someone playing on my drum?'

Rat yawned a big wide yawn. 'Drum? I don't think so.' He rubbed his eyes. 'But I was asleep, you know, so I heard nothing. Perhaps it was thunder over the mountain?'

'Perhaps,' said Cat and he went back out to the field.

Once again, the moment Cat was gone, Rat threw off the blankets and plucked up the drum. And, once again, he hit and thumped and pounded. He bished and bashed and boshed. But this time, by chance, he also happened to stroke it oh so gently with his paw.

Puurr-um puurr-um went the drum.

'That's it!' he cried. 'That's the special sound!'

Out in the fields, Cat heard the sound.

Puurr-um puurr-um. Puurr-um puurr-um.

'That's not thunder over the mountain!' he exclaimed. 'That's my drum!'

And he ran all the way home. But, again, Rat saw him coming; and, again, Cat found his friend in bed.

'My drum?' cried Cat. 'Was someone playing my drum?'

'What? No!' said Rat, sleepily. 'How could they? It would have woken me. Perhaps it was the wind in the trees.'

'Perhaps,' said Cat. But he didn't believe that for one moment. He left, but this time he didn't head back to the field. No. This time, he snuck round the back of the house and in through the window. He hid. And from his hiding place, he watched as Rat sprang out of bed, picked up the drum, and, dancing, began to play. As he danced, Rat sang:

My drum, my drum, my lovely drum.
I make it sing, *Puurr-um puurr-um.*
My drum, my drum, my lovely drum.
I fooled that Cat 'cause he's so dumb!

Cat could take it no longer.

'Rat! You tricked me!' he roared angrily. He jumped out from his hiding place and tried to grab Rat's tail. But the rodent was too fast. He swerved out of the way.

'Argh!' wailed Rat. 'Cat, I was only playing! It's just a drum!'

'You tricked me! You lied!'

Round and around the little hut they ran: round the chairs and round the table, round the dresser and round the bed.

'Give me the drum!'

'No!'

'Give me the drum!'

'No!'

Finally, Rat snagged his foot on the mat and stumbled. He fell to the ground. Cat, looming over him, opened his mouth wide, about to pounce. Rat, thinking fast, threw the drum into Cat's gaping jaws and down his throat. While Cat coughed and spluttered, Rat made his getaway, never to be seen again.

Cat, astounded, realised he had swallowed his drum. Then, from somewhere inside, he heard a familiar noise.

Puurr-um puurr-um. Puurr-um puurr-um.

The drum was playing inside him.

Puurr-um puurr-um. Puurr-um puurr-um.

How the Cat Came to Be

Now, from that day forth, Cat had no need to worry about who had his drum, for he carried it with him always, way down deep. But, if you are lucky, and if you are kind, Cat will *sometimes* let you play his drum. But you must never, ever play it roughly. No, you must always remember to stroke it oh so gently. And then, maybe, just maybe, you'll hear the tiny drum.

Puurr-um puurr-um. Puurr-um puurr-um
Puurr-um puurr-um. Puurr-um puurr-um.

Why Cats Always Wash after Eating

· Belgian ·

Cats are fastidious creatures. One of the cleanest of animals, they use their rough tongues to remove debris from their fur, while their forepaws are used (with that charming and characteristic mannerism) to wash their face and behind their ears. This fussiness, this attention to their appearance, helps lend cats their air of dignity and self-importance. This Belgian story, first published in English in 1918 but based on a piece of traditional oral folklore, explains how they learned their cleaning habits.

Belgium, incidentally, has a festival dedicated to cats, Kattenstoet. The triennial parade takes place in Ypres and honours a reputed medieval tradition of chucking cats from the Cloth Hall's tower. Quite why they did this is uncertain: possibly to rid themselves of evil spirits (for cats were associated with witchcraft), or possibly because the cats who guarded the cloth from rodents were not needed in spring, when the wool had been sold.

Thankfully, in the modern festival the only cats thrown from the belfry tower are cuddly toys.

One fine morning a tabby cat lay sunning itself on the grass, wondering what to do with its day.

'Should I go and explore the woods?' it thought. 'Or make friends with that pretty tortoiseshell next door? Or perhaps I could look for a nice juicy meal for breakfast?'

All the options were so tempting, however, that the cat couldn't make up its mind. Lost in thought, it lay completely still, daydreaming of woods, and tortoiseshells and breakfasts. In fact, it lay *so* still that an unsuspecting sparrow failed to notice its presence. The bird landed on the lawn and, looking for worms, hopped right past the cat.

'Hello? What's this?' thought the tabby, grinning. 'Looks like my decision's been made for me: a nice juicy breakfast it is!'

And, quick as lightning, the cat shot across the lawn and pinned the bird to the ground with its paw. It was just about to tuck in, when the bird spoke up.

'Really!' the sparrow tutted. 'Where are your manners?'

'My manners?' said the cat, insulted, for cats pride themselves on their good breeding. 'There's nothing wrong with my manners!'

'But you haven't washed yourself!' said the bird. 'Don't you know that kings and queens always wash before eating – and so does the king's cat.'

'The king's cat, eh?' said the cat, intrigued. 'Washes before eating, does he?'

'Without fail,' the sparrow assured him, nodding sombrely. 'Won't eat so much as a crumb without a clean.'

'Is that so?' mused the cat. 'I won't have my manners shown up by anyone – not even the king's cat.'

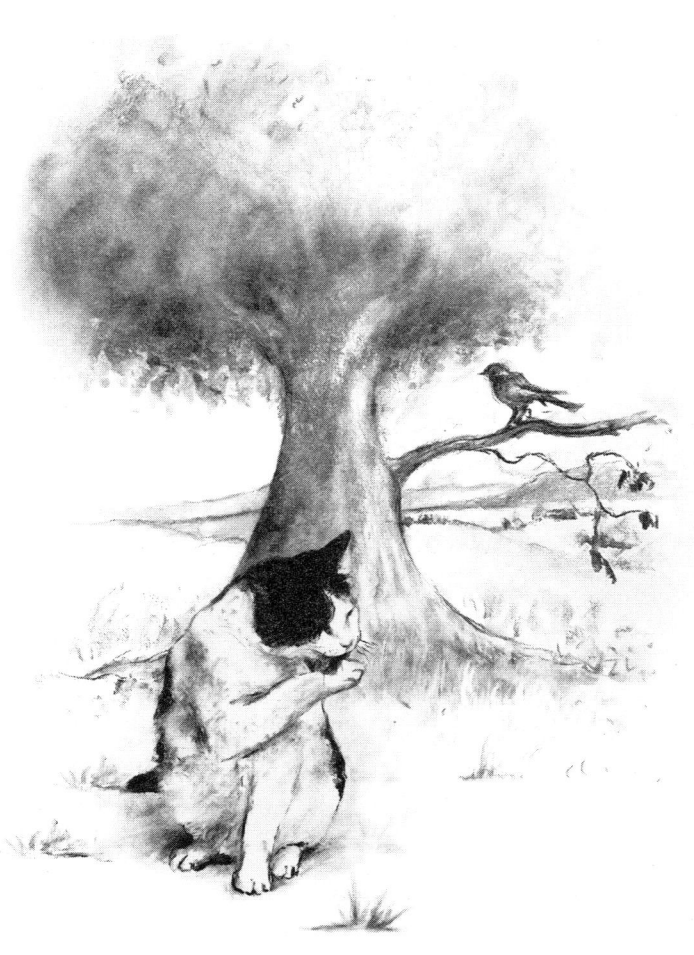

It dropped the sparrow and set about licking its paws, washing its face, and giving its whiskers a good spruce. When it had finished, the cat looked up to find the bird had escaped. It had fluttered to the top of an oak tree, far out of reach.

'Well,' muttered the cat, feeling irritated with itself. 'I won't make *that* mistake again.'

And that is why, from that day forth, cats always wash *after* eating.

Why the Dog Hates the Cat

· Chinese ·

The dog is the age-old enemy of the cat, at least in fiction and folklore. In this ancient Chinese story, a version of which was first published in English by Norman Hinsdale Pitman in 1919, the cat and the dog are initially friends, until the cat's act of betrayal changes everything forever. Cats are actually the more popular of the two in China, making it one of the few regions of the world where the cat outnumbers the dog.

Undoubtedly, the two species do fight in real life. There are numerous reasons for this: a lack of socialisation, a negative early experience, a traumatised cat, the dog's instinct to give chase. However, the idea that cats and dogs are permanently at each other's throats is a myth. Often, the two co-exist perfectly harmoniously. Some, in fact, are the best of friends. And, despite the popular image of the bullying dog chasing the put-upon cat, when they do squabble, it is more often the cat who plays the aggressor.

In this story, also known as 'The Golden Beetle', the cat is certainly to blame.

It had been a bleak winter and a widow and her son were suffering. The roof of their tiny cottage leaked, the larder was empty and, worst of all, the lad had lost his job. Every day he tried to scrape together enough for a meagre meal – a bit of soup, perhaps, or a bowl of rice – but times were tough, and many were the nights when they went to bed hungry. It was hardest for their pets, a cat and a dog. The poor cat, once so proud of its thick ginger fur, was now mangy and shabby. While the dog – a great grey mongrel – had grown skinny and weak.

But the widow and her son never gave up. They still had each other, they still had hope, and they believed that better times would come.

One day, when the lad was out looking for work, an old priest arrived at the door. He told the woman that she had been an excellent mother and that her boy had been an excellent son. He had come to reward them. Handing her a golden beetle, he said, 'Keep it close, for you will never go hungry as long as it is yours. Place the beetle in a pot and say the name of the food you wish to eat. Then the food will appear.'

Well, the woman didn't really believe the man, of course, for his tale was far too good to be true. But she was desperate. So, the moment he had left, she dropped the beetle into the pot, saying, 'Dumplings, dumplings, dumplings.'

When she took off the lid, she was agog! The pot was brimming with fragrant, mouth-watering dumplings. She ate until she couldn't manage another bite. The rest was given to the cat and the dog, who were delighted with their change in fortune.

'Delicious!' purred the cat.

'Wonderful!' barked the dog.

That evening, the son returned home exhausted and depressed. 'Another day with no food in our bellies,' he moaned.

Why the Dog Hates the Cat

But his mother told him to sit at the table.

'What's the point?' he grumbled. 'We've no food.'

'Just sit!' insisted the mother. Then she dropped the golden beetle into the pot, and said, 'Dumplings, dumplings, dumplings.'

'Oh, mother!' the son cried, with tears in his eyes. 'Have your wits deserted you? You can't make food with words!'

But when his mother placed a bowlful of dumplings before him, he soon changed his tune.

From then on, the mother, the son, the cat and the dog dined as they had never dined before: noodles, rice, chicken and beef; spicy, savoury, salty and sweet; soups and puddings and biscuits and teas – everything and anything they could think of to eat. Soon the lad grew strong, and the animals grew fat.

However, with the family's happiness came pride. They wanted to show off their good fortune and they invited their neighbours to dinner. One of these neighbours, jealous of the richness of the widow's meals, watched her with beady eyes. She spotted the golden beetle being dropped into the pot.

'Hmm, it must be a magical charm,' the neighbour thought bitterly. 'Why should she have all the luck? I'll steal it; then *I* can have these dumplings for dinner each night.'

The next day the widow and her son went out to spend the day at the fair. When the neighbour was certain they had left, she crept into the empty house and stole the golden beetle from the cupboard. The animals made no trouble. The dog snored before the fire and the cat, full after a hearty lunch, idled in a patch of sun.

How the Cat Came to Be

A little later, the widow and the lad returned. It was dinner-time and the woman headed straight to the cupboard to fetch the beetle. But an awful shock awaited her.

'Ah! Disaster!' she exclaimed, when she found it missing. 'Calamity! A thief has taken our golden beetle! Son, whatever shall we do? We'll starve again!'

Alas, it was true. The days of plenty were gone. Once more, the son went out each morning, hoping to earn a coin or two. And, once more, the cat and the dog roamed the streets looking for scraps to eat.

'I'm fed up!' complained the cat one day, sucking an old pigeon bone it had found. 'In fact, I'm more than fed up! My tummy grumbles and my legs are weak. I want the good days back!'

'Don't we all?' the dog replied. 'Do you think I *like* being hungry? But unless you know *how* to get the good days back, there's no point in griping.'

'But I *do* know how,' insisted the cat. 'Do you remember the day the golden beetle went missing? Well, I saw our neighbour sneak into the house and take something from the cupboard. And we haven't had a good meal since!'

'Our neighbour? A thief!' growled the dog, springing up. 'Why, I'll bite her so hard she'll rue the day she wronged us!'

'Calm yourself,' said the cat. 'You're being ridiculous. Revenge is a human emotion. We're only interested in getting back the beetle – and, with it, our grub.'

The cat and the dog sat down together and carefully made a

Why the Dog Hates the Cat

plan to steal back the beetle. The neighbour lived on the far side of the village and the quickest route was across the river. The cat rode upon the dog's back, for it hated to get wet.

When they reached the neighbour's house, the cat scrambled over the garden wall into the courtyard. At that moment, an unsuspecting rat scurried past. Quick as a scorpion, the cat pinned the rat with its fearsome claws.

'Oh, please! Show mercy!' squeaked the rat. 'I have forty-seven children to feed!'

'Answer my questions then,' whispered the cat. 'Have the household been eating well? Have you seen a golden beetle?'

'Yes! Yes!' the rat squealed, piteously. 'They've dined as never before: great piles of food appear from thin air. And, now you mention it, I *have* seen a golden beetle. They keep it hidden in the wall.'

'Just as I suspected,' spat the cat. 'Fetch me the beetle and I'll spare your pitiful life,' it told the rat. 'But double-cross me and you'll regret it.'

A little later, the rat returned with the beetle.

'Excellent,' purred the cat. 'Now scram before I change my mind.'

The rat fled, and the cat returned to the dog, the beetle in its mouth.

Crossing the river again, the dog, a worryguts, said, 'Please keep the beetle safe. Whatever you do, don't drop it!'

The cat was annoyed. 'Of course I'll keep it safe. Do you think I'm an idiot?'

Halfway across, however, a fish arced out of the water. The cat's instincts took over. Unable to stop itself, the cat lunged at the fish, catching it in its jaws. And as the cat opened its mouth, the beetle tumbled into the river.

'Nitwit!' barked the dog. 'Nincompoop! We're lost without that charm!'

And the pair began to squabble and fight, calling each other the most hurtful names they knew.

'Stop it!' grumbled a frog on a nearby leaf. 'You're behaving like *people*! I'll fetch the knick-knack for you, if it ends this bother and nonsense.'

And it dived into the silty river and emerged with the golden beetle.

Their treasure returned, the cat and the dog continued home in frosty silence. When they arrived at the house the door was shut and the widow and her son were in their beds, too feeble to rise. No amount of barking could raise them. Finding an open window, the dog tried to squeeze through but was too big. So, the cat hopped up and slipped inside. Then it dropped the trinket on the mother's belly and licked her face until she woke.

The woman wept with joy when she saw the golden beetle. 'Was this your doing?' she asked the cat. 'Oh, you dear, dear thing! Oh, what a clever creature!'

She made a humungous breakfast for her and her son. Then they showered the cat with kisses and cuddles. More importantly, however, they gave it a steaming bowl of delicious dumplings.

Why the Dog Hates the Cat

But there were no kisses or cuddles or dumplings for the dog. He was left in the garden, famished and freezing.

After eating its fill, the cat sauntered outside. 'What a tip-top meal,' it said, cleaning its paws. 'Really quite scrumptious!' Then it added, with a nasty little laugh, 'Such a shame there wasn't any for you.'

'Why, you scoundrel! You traitor!' snarled the dog. Incensed, it grabbed the cat in its jaws and shook it until it was dead.

The dog spread word of the cat's infamy. Soon every dog in the land knew what fickle, untrustworthy beasts they were. And, from that day to this, the dog hates the cat, and the cat hates the dog, and they fight wherever they meet.

How the Manx Cat Lost Its Tail

· Manx ·

The Manx cat originates on the Isle of Man. While they have round heads and hind legs longer than their front legs (lending them a pronounced hump), these are not the characteristics that made them famous. Rather, they are known around the world for one remarkable feature: their lack of a tail. (Although, in fact, Manx cats – or stubbin, *as they're called on the island – can range from having a short tail to no tail at all.)*

There have been numerous explanations for how the Manx cat gained its distinctive appearance: the first cat on the island was a tailless survivor of a shipwreck; Viking invaders butchered cats for their tails, believing them to be good luck, forcing mother cats to chew off their kittens' appendages; they are the descendants of the coupling of a cat and a rabbit; a lord tried to tax cats' tails, but was thwarted when the canny islanders lopped them all off. Some spoilsports even claim that it is a natural mutation caused by a dominant gene with a high penetrance.

However, the explanation in the following story seems the most interesting. A traditional Manx tale, it has, in the words of Sophia Morrison, one of its early collectors, been 'handed down by word of mouth from father to son' for generations.

God was unhappy. His creation, humankind, had displeased him. It had been ten generations since Adam and Eve had left their paradise, and Man had spread out across the Earth. But everywhere God looked he witnessed violence and wickedness, depravity and sin.

'Well,' he shrugged, 'you can't get everything right. Best get rid of this and start again.'

He resolved to send a great flood to wipe out humanity.

God had, however, noticed one man more noble and righteous than the rest. The man's name was Noah and God decided to spare him and his family.

He appeared before the old man.

'Noah,' God said, 'I am to send a flood. It will last for forty days and forty nights and none but you and yours shall survive. For you shall build a great boat – an ark – and in this boat you will sail across the waters with your sons and their wives. And you will take two of each animal – a male and female – for the world will need repopulating once the waters have receded.'

Now, Noah was rather put out by this news. But he did as he was told. He and his sons built a huge boat, large enough to fit two of each animal in the world. It was laborious work, and they only just finished in time, for no sooner was the ark completed than the first drops of rain began to fall.

Noah summoned the animals to him. Slowly, they filed onto the boat, two by two. The dogs came and the cows came; the lions came and the giraffes came; the eagles and the woodlice and the aardvarks and the bears came. Soon the ark was a riot of mess and noise. The monkeys swung on the elephants' trunks. The rhinos poked the zebras on their bottoms. The caterpillars tickled the

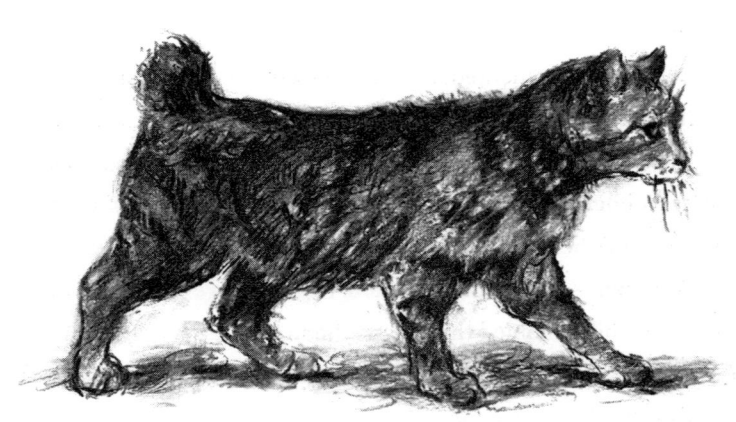

orangutans' toes. Birds flapped, insects scuttled, lizards lounged. Everywhere Noah looked there was fur and feathers, tusks and tails. And the smell! It was beyond all imagining.

Noah studied his list, checking all the passengers were on board. He ticked off the animals one by one.

They were all present – all except one cat, a brownish tabby, who was busy hunting mice.

'Get a move on!' yelled Noah. 'It's time to go!'

'I won't be long!' the cat called, chasing a mouse round a table.

'One sec!' she shouted, scurrying down the cellar steps.

'In a jiffy!' she yelled, snapping and grabbing at the pest.

Well, finally, Noah could wait no longer, for the rain was falling in buckets and the floodwater rising. He began to heave shut the ark's heavy door.

And then – in the nick of time – the sopping cat leapt from the water and scrabbled through the hatch, a dead mouse hanging from its jaws.

But, at the very same moment, Noah slammed the door, trapping the cat's long, elegant tail and severing it from the poor creature's behind.

And that, I'm afraid, is why the Manx cat has no tail.

Why the Cat Kills Rats

· Nigerian ·

Cats are not highly esteemed in Nigeria, a country that much prefers dogs. As in many areas of the world, cats are too yoked to witchcraft and black magic to be widely loved here. But this traditional folk tale from southern Nigeria explains the enmity between the cat and the rat, traditionally seen as great foes.

Cats do hunt rats, although not nearly as often or as successfully as one might think. Rats are rather large prey for a cat (they can weigh ten times more than a mouse) and so only the largest, or most desperate, cat will usually tackle them.

Once there was a king who kept a cat as his housekeeper. The cat worked until he was weary, for the palace had a hundred rooms and the king demanded a hundred dishes with each meal. The cat's only helper was a rat – and the rat was really no help at all. He was in love with the king's daughter and spent his days mooning after her, whispering poetry in her ear.

The rat longed to give the princess a present. But he didn't have a penny to his name. So, in desperation, he stole a purple pear from the pantry and gave it to the girl.

Unfortunately, the cat was a real stickler about his job. At the end of each week, he counted all the food in the stores and pantries; and, this week, he noticed that a purple pear was missing.

Why the Cat Kills Rats

The cat was outraged. He rushed around the palace, interviewing suspects, following clues, finding evidence. It wasn't long before he discovered that the princess had been spotted eating a purple pear.

'I got it from the rat,' admitted the girl, blushing, when she was asked. 'He's a dear little fellow and likes to give me gifts.'

The cat went straight to the king and told him of the rat's crime. The king, who had a horrible temper, sent the girl to her room. Then he had the rat thrown out of the palace and banished from the kingdom.

Finally, the king turned to the cat, his faithful housekeeper.

'You have served me well, old friend,' said the king. 'But that rascally rat was your responsibility. Therefore, you must leave my service and never darken my door again.'

The cat was heartbroken. He blamed the rat for the loss of his position. So, in revenge, he killed him and skinned him and swallowed him down.

And that is why cats kill rats.

2

The Mysterious Cat

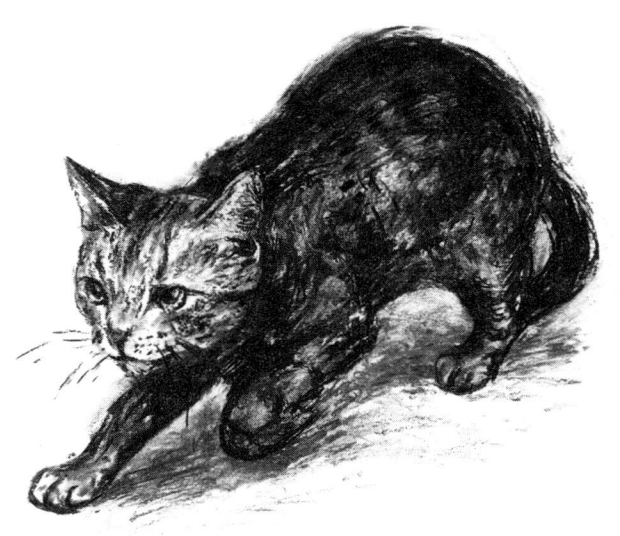

Cats are the most mysterious of creatures. They are animals not entirely of this world. Though they share our mundane lives, they belong on another plane of existence, one more magical, more mystical than ours. While dogs are solid and stolid – beasts of earth and sunlight – cats are shrouded in shadow, illuminated by moonlight. Crepuscular, cats are most active at dawn and dusk. Together with their shining, orb-like eyes, this night-time rambling may explain the age-old connection between cats and the moon.

In many cultures, cats were associated with moon goddesses: the Ancient Egyptian Bastet; the Roman Diana; Artemis and Hecate of Ancient Greece. The Greeks believed that cats' eyes waxed and waned with the moon. In West Africa, cats cause lunar eclipses by nibbling the moon's rim. In China, they steal moonbeams. To Cornelius Agrippa, a sixteenth-century alchemist, their forms changed with the moon, making them lunar animals, valuable to magicians.

One has only to observe these magical, moonlit creatures to understand why cats are held to be supernatural. There is so much in their movements and habits that make them otherworldly. Cats appear and disappear at will. They blend with shadows. They slink and creep. They move silently, entering and leaving rooms unnoticed. Cats even look supernatural, with eyes that glow in the moonlight, bodies that stretch and shrink into preposterous shapes, and the stealthy prowl of a miniature panther.

And just like panthers, cats are killing machines. For tame as they seem, cats remain part wild. Millennia of domestication have not dulled their hunting instincts – or their claws. Inside every pet cat there remains a predator. This is the cat feared by birds and mice. But it is visible, in flickers and flashes, to humans too: in playful bites, in warning scratches, in teeth bared to tail-tugging toddlers.

This hint of menace and unpredictability only adds to their otherness – an otherness that led numerous civilisations to judge them divine. Most memorably, two of the ancient Egyptians' most prominent deities, Sekhmet and Bastet, possessed feline heads. These goddesses were, in fact, aspects of the same being. As a lion, Sekhmet was a warrior goddess, representing chaos, war and the burning desert sun. When in cat form, she became Bastet: goddess of protection, pregnancy and good health. As the Egyptians recognised, this perfectly represented the twofold nature of cats: domestic and gentle on the one hand; agents of chaos and violence on the other.

The ancient Egyptians' veneration of cats extended beyond these goddesses. Even household cats were deemed sacred. In part, this was a show of respect to Bastet. But cats had also earned the Egyptians' admiration in their own right: by hunting rodents they prevented disease and protected crops; by killing snakes they saved lives; and their combination of elegance and aggression made them figures of fascination and awe. Consequently, the ancient Egyptians made every effort to honour their cats: killing a cat was punishable by death; exporting one was forbidden; and when a cat died, it was customary for its owner to shave their eyebrows. Cats, evidently, were loved, not merely revered. And this reverence continued in death. Archaeologists have discovered vast cemeteries of mummified cats, with 200,000 unearthed in one cemetery alone.

Sekhmet and Bastet are far from the only deities associated with cats. In ancient Egypt, Mut, Kek, Mafdet and Nefertem could all adopt the form of a cat. Artemis – goddess of the wild, of hunting and of children, and the ancient Greek analogue of Bastet – became a cat on occasion, as did her Roman parallel, Diana. Other deities credited with appearing as cats include the Lithuanian fire spirit Gabija, the ancient Chinese god of wealth, Cai Shen, and Shashthi, Hindu goddess of children.

Numerous other gods, meanwhile, though not themselves feline, were heavily associated with cats. In Welsh mythology, two white cats served Ceridwen, goddess of wisdom. Cats were a symbol of Venus, Roman goddess of love, who was often depicted with black cats at her feet. Black cats were also symbolic of Hecate, Greek goddess of witchcraft and the moon.

Largely due to their connection with Hecate and Diana, cats became coupled with witchcraft, tainting them with an unfortunate whiff of sulphur and black magic. To the medieval mind, they were witches, demons and familiar spirits – a relationship that survives in the popular imagination to this day, ensuring that to many cats will forever be regarded as magical and otherworldly.

Unsurprisingly, therefore, cats in fairy tales and folklore are often magical beasts. In the following stories we see cats who can speak and cats who can dance; cats who save and cats who kill; cursed cats and enchanted cats; fairy cats and royal cats; cats who offer fortunes, slay giants, and win kingdoms. In culture after culture, we find stories of cats with supernatural abilities.

So, when you curl up of an evening in front of the television, remember that the creature stretched across your knees is not just a humble moggy, not just a coddled and pampered pet – no, that feline is a supernatural being, terrible and divine. It can shapeshift and turn invisible; eat the moon and control the sea; bring the best of fortune or the worst of luck. It may be a witch or a demon; a princess or a king. It may pull the chariot of a goddess or represent one on Earth. Or perhaps, just possibly, you have a god or goddess itself purring on your lap.

No wonder it expects your devotion.

The Little White Cat

· Irish ·

Cats feature prominently in the fairy tales and folklore of Ireland. In one myth, two goddesses, sisters named Clíodhna and Aibell, both fall in love with Caiov, a handsome prince. Discovering that Caiov prefers Aibell, Clíodhna lures her sister to a cave and transforms her into a white cat. Clíodhna is then free to marry the prince. When the prince discovers his wife's crime, however, she is banished from his side. Aibell, meanwhile, lives on in the cave as a white cat, surrounded by treasure, returning to her true form for only one week each year.

In another tale, the sons of Dian Cecht, god of healing, replace a man's eye with the eye of a cat. This causes all sorts of problems: when the man tries to sleep, his eye is searching for birds and rodents, but when he tries to concentrate on human affairs, his eye drifts off to sleep.

In yet another story, Irusan, King of the Cats, fatally quarrels with Seanchan, the Chief Bard, after the bard criticises his rat-killing skills.

The following fairy tale is based on a version collected in 1890 by Edmund Leamy, a politician and writer, but its origins are older and uncertain.

Once upon a time a giant kidnapped a princess and took her to live in his castle. He gave her the most delicious food and the finest clothes, and she had a troupe of dwarves to wait on her. But her door was guarded by a hundred monstrous hounds, and she was warned that if she ever tried to escape, they would tear her limb from limb.

The princess wept. She was in love with a fine young man, the Prince of the Silver Run, and feared she'd never see him again. And when the giant said she had to marry *him*, she wept some more.

She went to the window, hoping to climb out. But the tower was nearly as high as the clouds, and at the bottom were the ferocious dogs, waiting to tear her apart. There was no way out.

Then, in a nearby tree, she saw a fluffy white cat purring on a branch.

'Oh, you dear little thing!' she said. 'Come here to me.'

And the cat hopped in through the window. The lonely princess swept the animal into her arms and covered it with kisses.

'Princess, the giant has gone away to fight a war,' said the cat, 'but when he returns, say you will marry him—'

'What!' snorted the princess. 'I'd rather die than marry that brute!'

'I know,' said the cat, patiently. 'Let me finish. Just *say* you'll marry him, but on one condition: that his dwarves gather the fairy dew from a fine misty morning and spin it into three balls the size of these.' And he pulled three balls, as small as peas, from his ear, and handed them to her. One was red, one yellow and one blue.

'They're not very large,' said the princess, doubtfully. 'It won't take the dwarves long.'

'It will take them three months and three days,' the cat replied.

The cat jumped onto the window ledge and said, 'When you see a prince on this branch, throw him the three balls. But don't say a word, for otherwise the hounds will hear.'

And then the cat was gone.

The next day, the giant returned from his war. He went straight to the princess.

'Are you ready for our wedding?' he growled.

The princess said: 'Nearly. I *will* marry you, lord giant, but on one condition. Your dwarves must gather the fairy dew from a fine misty morning and spin it into three such balls.'

And she held out her palm, displaying the balls.

The giant guffawed so loudly the windows rattled. 'Why, that will take them no time at all! I'll agree – because we'll be married by this time tomorrow.'

But he was no longer laughing the next day, when he saw how little fairy dew his dwarves had gathered. And by the morning after that, when they still had no more dew than a pixie's tear, he was raging, for he saw he had been tricked.

Meanwhile, the cat visited the Prince of the Silver Run. The poor man was heartbroken. He loved the princess and knew not where the giant had taken her.

'My prince,' said the cat, 'I have discovered where your true love is hidden.'

'What! Where?' cried the prince. 'Tell me at once!'

'In the giant's tower, guarded by a hundred hounds who will eat her if she tries to escape.'

The prince sprang up. 'I will kill the giant and slay the hounds!' he scowled, drawing his sword.

'I think not,' said the cat. 'The giant cannot be killed by any sword made by human hands, and those hounds will tear you limb from limb.'

'Then what *am* I to do?' asked the prince.

'There is but one sword in all the world that can kill the giant,' said the cat, 'and that sword resides on an island that no man has ever set foot upon.'

'Tell me how to reach it!' cried the prince.

'Very well – but you must follow my instructions to the letter,' said the cat. 'Go to the tower and climb to the highest window. The princess will throw three balls to you. But don't say a word, for otherwise the hounds will hear.'

The prince galloped to the tower. He climbed the tree to the princess's window. Leaning out, the princess tossed the three balls to him and blew him three kisses. But, remembering what the cat had told them, neither spoke a word.

Back at his palace, the prince found the cat sitting by the seashore.

'Take the red ball,' the cat said, 'and unravel a thread. Hold the thread while you drop the ball in the water. Then, when the ball has floated so far it can no longer be seen, pull on the thread.'

The Mysterious Cat

The prince did as he was told. The ball bobbed away on the waves, unspooling, and floated into the distance. Then the prince gave the thread a tug. Far away, he saw a flash of silver. Encouraged, he kept pulling, until a little silver ship was hauled right up to the shore.

'This boat will take you to an island where no human has ever set foot. There you will find the sword that can slay the giant,' said the cat. 'You will also find one hundred cakes. These will subdue the hounds.'

The prince jumped into the boat and pushed away from the shore.

The cat called after him, 'Heed this: do not have a bite to eat nor a drop to drink, otherwise you will lose all memory of the princess.'

'Impossible!' scoffed the prince. 'Only death could make me forget my one true love.'

For three days and three nights, the prince sailed over unknown seas. The waves were rough, and the wind was bitter, and the prince grew weak and hungry. He had begun to fear the voyage would never end when, early on the morning of the fourth day, the silver boat made land on a small island. The island was blanketed in exotic fruit trees. In his hunger, the prince forgot the cat's warning. He plucked a piece of fruit from a branch and ate it greedily. Precisely as the cat had foretold, the prince lost all memory of the princess.

The prince wandered this way and that across the island, as in a dream. After a while, he heard the strains of a sweet,

The Little White Cat

mysterious music, which he followed to a glade. Here, he found three young women strumming on their harps. They led the prince to a golden palace.

It was the home of a king and queen. Their daughter was nearly as beautiful as the princess in the tower. The forgetful prince saw this new princess and was bewitched. Before long, he and the king's daughter had arranged to be married.

On the eve of the wedding, however, the little white cat hopped through the window. He settled on the prince's lap. At the touch of the cat's fur, the young man's memory flooded back: he remembered the silver boat; he remembered the giant and the hounds; but, most of all, he remembered the beautiful princess locked inside the tower.

'Oh, cat, help me!' he cried. 'I must reach the island and find the sword able to slay the giant – for I must rescue my one true love! Tell me what to do!'

'Drop the yellow ball into the sea, and summon a boat as you did before,' said the cat. 'But don't, whatever you do, look upon the face of a single person until you are free of the island.'

As soon as morning broke, the prince set off for the water. Leaving the castle gate, the guards called to him, but he did not turn and look upon their faces. Then, passing through the glade, he heard the harps of the three young women, but he did not turn and look upon their faces. Finally, as he stepped onto the boat, which he had summoned with the ball, he heard the princess call to him. But, tempted though he was, he did not turn and look upon her face.

The Mysterious Cat

As he guided the boat out to sea, he heard a blood-chilling scream, so loud and sharp the prince clamped his hands to his ears. He spun around. The ravishing princess, the three harpists, and the golden castle had all vanished. Instead, he saw fire-breathing serpents, hideous and odious.

He fled as fast as he could.

For three days and three nights, the silver boat skimmed over unknown seas until, on the morning of the fourth day, it found land. The island was covered with juicy red berries. The prince, so hungry he feared he would die, crammed them into his mouth. As soon as he did so, however, the memory of the princess disappeared once more from his mind.

Three giants lumbered from a thicket. One picked up the prince by the legs and dangled him in the air.

'What's this then?' she said.

'Dunno,' said another, scratching his chin. 'It's a runty little thing!'

'Some kinda rat, perhaps,' said the third.

'Insolent brute!' shouted their captive. 'I'm not a rat! I'm a prince! Unhand me, this instant!'

The giants bickered over what to do with their find. One wanted him as a pet. Another thought he'd make a fine dishrag. But the third, a cook, said he should be fattened up and fed to the king.

The prince was taken to the cook's kitchen, where she plied him with cakes and sweets and chocolate trifle. Finally, when he

The Little White Cat

was plump enough, the cook said he was to be eaten by the king the very next day.

The prince was in despair. How was he to escape? But then he felt the soft touch of fluffy fur rub against his leg. Looking down, he saw the little white cat. Immediately, he remembered the princess in the tower.

The cat said, 'You have failed. Again. But for the sake of the princess, I will give you one more chance to reach the island and claim the sword. Tomorrow morning, tell the giant you desire a final look at the sea before you die. Once there, use the blue ball to summon the boat.'

The prince did as the cat suggested. The giant took him to the beach, and the prince called the boat. Then, before the giant knew what was happening, the young man had leapt onto the boat and sailed away into the distance.

For three days and three nights the prince sailed the boat over unknown sees, wild and windy, until he landed on an island of extraordinary beauty. Though hungry and thirsty, he did not have a bite to eat nor a drop to drink. Instead, he ambled through a sun-dappled wood to a rich valley, where he found a white castle.

In the castle was a great circular room with a thousand pillars, on each of which sat a cat. The cat on the central pillar was the prince's old friend.

'I am the King of the Cats and this is my castle,' explained the little white cat. 'Take these gifts,' he said, gesturing to a wondrous sword and a basket of cakes. 'The sword is magical, for it was forged not by human hands but by feline paws. It is the only sword in all the world with the power to slay the giant. The cakes, meanwhile, will get rid of the dogs. Now,' continued the king, 'return to the tower. You have no time to lose. It has been three months and two days since the dwarves begun to spin the fairy dew. Tomorrow they will finish the final ball, and the princess will be forced to marry the giant.'

The prince did as he was told. His boat seemed to fly over the waves and, before long, he landed on the giant's shore.

At the tower, the gargantuan hounds stood in his way, growling and baring their teeth. But the prince threw the cakes to the dogs, who munched on the enchanted treats. They soon fell sound asleep.

'Show yourself, giant!' the prince shouted, banging the cat's sword on his shield. 'Come out and fight!'

The mighty door of the tower groaned open. Out stomped the giant, as tall as a tree and as heavy as ten elephants.

'Who dares disturb me on my wedding day?' he boomed.

'I am the Prince of the Silver Run,' replied the prince. 'You stole my princess; prepare to die.'

The giant let out a bark of anger like a rumble of thunder and charged towards the prince. But the prince bounded up the giant's leg. With a tremendous leap, he thrust his sword through the giant's heart. The giant roared and writhed and stamped in pain; then, like a falling oak, toppled dead to the floor.

The joyful princess ran from the tower and jumped into the prince's arms.

The Little White Cat

Before the month was out, the prince and the princess celebrated their wedding – with their dear friend the King of the Cats as their guest of honour. And then, of course, the royal couple returned to their palace and lived happily ever after.

The Colony of Cats

· Italian ·

This Italian tale, believed to be of Sicilian roots but of uncertain age and origin, features not one cat, but a whole colony of the creatures. They are led by the kindly Father Gatto ('cat' in Italian). To the deserving, he is generous and wise; to the undeserving, rather severe and intimidating. A warning, perhaps, to always treat cats with suitable respect.

Italy really is home to a number of cat colonies. In this cat-loving country, groups of feral cats have a legal right to live undisturbed wherever they choose, with the authorities obliged to feed, spay and neuter them. Consequently, you will see strays dwelling unmolested among the country's picturesque ruins, with famous colonies in Milan, Sicily and Venice.

It is in Rome, however, that cats have made themselves most at home. The city houses an estimated 4,000 colonies, which wander freely among such iconic sites as the Colosseum, the Spanish Steps, and the Baths of Caracalla. The most notable colony is the Torre Argentina Cat Sanctuary. There, located between four temples and the remains of Pompey's Theatre, some 250 cats bask amid Rome's ancient and distinguished ruins.

Once there was a colony of cats who lived in a large, rambling house. They enjoyed a life of great comfort, with a servant who cooked and shopped and kept the place spick and span. However,

The Colony of Cats

the cats were so horribly bossy that the servant was at the end of her tether. There were only so many ears she could scratch and backs she could stroke. And there simply weren't enough hours in the day for all the litter trays, meals and medicines. They even had the poor woman on her hands and knees helping them catch mice. One day she threw her pinny to the ground and stormed out, never to return.

Later that morning a young woman named Lizina knocked on the cats' door. Her mother had cruelly beaten her with a broom and she had run away, but she had nowhere else to go, so she begged the cats to allow her to work for them. She had a kind face and a gentle manner and the cats agreed that she could stay.

At first, Lizina found the job difficult. There were so many dozens of cats that she could hardly keep track of them all. And the house was in a constant state of confusion, for there were cats sleeping everywhere she looked: on pianos and wardrobes, under tables and beds, in cupboards and cabinets and clocks. And, of course, when they weren't sleeping it was even worse, for then they were making mischief of one kind or another – squabbling noisily or pinching food, playing chase or getting stuck in trees.

But, in time, she learned each cat's name; and she learned how to brush the fur from the carpet, and how to make mouse lasagne, and how to plump the cushions in their baskets – and a hundred and one other chores. What's more, she nursed the old, sick cats so gently and played with the young kittens so adorably, that all the cats grew to love her.

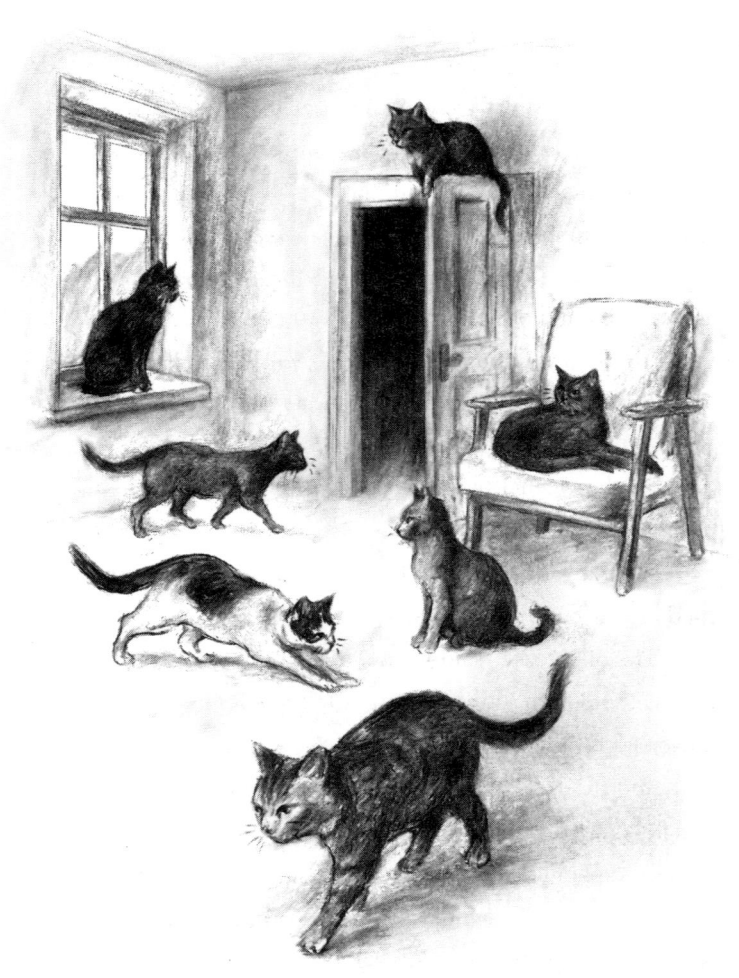

An elderly grey-and-white tomcat named Father Gatto was especially fond of Lizina. One day he noticed that the girl's eyes were red.

'What is wrong, Lizina?' he asked, licking the tears from her cheek. 'Why is your face leaking?'

'Because I miss my mother and sister,' sobbed the girl.

'But they were unkind to you, were they not?' asked Father Gatto, puzzled by the notion.

'Well, yes,' admitted Lizina. 'But they are the only family I have. And, kind or unkind, I love them still.'

'Ah, then you must go and visit them, my dear,' said the old cat, impressed by the girl's sweet and forgiving nature. 'But first, I'd like to give you a little gift.'

He showed her two large pots. One was full of oil, the other of liquid gold.

'Now, my dear, you can be dipped in one of these pots,' said Father Gatto. 'Which one shall it be?'

'The oil, please,' said Lizina, blushing modestly.

Father Gatto tutted. 'You are too humble, Lizina,' he said. 'If anyone has earned good fortune, it is you.'

And he dunked her in the pot of precious metal. As if by magic, Lizina's clothes were made of shining gold. Her hair was black, and her cheeks were rosy, but otherwise she was as bright and golden as the noonday sun. Even the golden pockets in her golden dress overflowed with golden coins.

'Run along home, dear,' said Father Gatto. 'But please remember this: when you hear the cock crow, turn to face it;

The Mysterious Cat

but if you hear the bray of a donkey, make sure you look away, whatever you do.'

Lizina raced home, for she was longing to see her family. On the way, she heard the crow of the cock. She spun to look at the bird.

A golden star appeared on her forehead!

She continued on her way. Before long, she heard the bray of a donkey. Remembering Father Gatto's words, she glanced away, shielding her eyes with her hand.

Once Lizina reached home, her mother nearly fainted at the sight of her, overcome by her golden star and her shining clothes. They were a miserably poor family and the coins in the girl's pockets would save them from hunger. Now, instead of beating her with a broom, her mother smothered her with kisses. Lizina's sister, Peppina, however, was racked with jealousy.

'It's not fair!' she whined. 'Why should Lizina be so rich and beautiful, when I have nothing at all!'

She made up her mind to work for the cats and gain a fortune of her own.

When the cats learned that Peppina was Lizina's sister they were happy to take her in. But where Lizina was kind and gentle, Peppina was surly and rough; where Lizina was hard-working and modest, Peppina was lazy and vain. Soon the house was covered with filth. Worse, Peppina never nursed the old, sick cats nor played lovingly with the little kittens.

The cats were unhappy and complained to Father Gatto. He knew what had to be done.

The old cat showed Peppina the pots of oil and gold and asked in which she wished to be dipped.

'The gold! The gold!' squealed Peppina, clapping her hands.

The old cat frowned. 'You chose poorly,' he said slowly. 'You have not yet earned the gold.'

So, instead of the pot of gold, he dunked her in the pot of oil and threw her on the dirty floor, caking her from head to toe in dust and grime and cobwebs.

'Serves you right for not cleaning better!' said Father Gatto severely. 'You will leave our house this very second. But remember this: if you hear the bray of a donkey, make sure to turn towards it, whatever you do.'

Peppina fled crying. When she heard the donkey bray, she looked it in the eye. And a donkey's tail sprouted on her forehead!

When the girl returned home, her mother wailed to see her in such a sorry state. Between them, they managed to scrub off the muck, but try as they might, nothing could get rid of the tail.

Poor Lizina got the blame, for Peppina had always been their mother's favourite. She was beaten with the broom once more and thrown to the bottom of a well.

The next morning a prince arrived. You see, while Peppina had been living with the cats, the prince had happened to pass by the cottage. He and Lizina had fallen in love at first sight. Captivated by her beauty, the prince had asked her to be his wife, and she had accepted.

But Lizina's mother hoped to trick the prince into marrying Peppina instead. So, when the prince arrived, he found his bride's face hidden by a white veil. It was, in fact, Peppina, and the veil was to cover the donkey's tail.

The prince, not realising his mistake, helped his bride into the carriage. As they drove, they passed the house where the cats lived. The animals had learned of the abominable treatment of Lizina, however, and were lined up outside. They began to sing in screechy, untuneful voices:

> Prince, oh Prince, lift up that veil:
> You'll find a face with a donkey's tail.
> Prince, oh Prince, we're here to tell:
> Your fair Lizina is down the well.

The prince did lift up the veil. Instead of Lizina's pretty face he saw a hateful scowl; instead of a golden star he saw a drooping tail. Letting out a roar of anger, he ordered the coach to turn around. They tore back to the cottage, driving so fast the wheels made sparks on the cobblestones. Then, once there, the prince rescued Lizina from the darkness of the well.

A week later, the prince and Lizina were married at the royal palace. The greatest lords and ladies in the land attended, but none of the guests were more joyfully welcomed than kind Father Gatto and the colony of cats.

The White Cat

· French ·

In Britain, white cats are often considered to be bad luck – possibly, it has been surmised, because white is deemed to be the colour of ghosts. This is reflected in the various British superstitions surrounding white cats: having one in your house will bring poverty on you; bad luck will follow if one crosses your path; seeing one in the night-time is an ill omen; spotting one on the way to school means that trouble lies ahead.

However, in much of the world, white cats, unlike their black-furred companions, are considered good fortune – unsurprisingly, given white is traditionally a symbol of purity and innocence. In America, Japan, Russia and many parts of Europe, therefore, white cats are lucky charms.

In this French story – a literary fairy tale written by Madame d'Aulnoy in 1698 – the presence of a white cat proves a stroke of luck for the young prince.

In a far-off land there lived a king with three sons. The king was old and poorly. He knew that soon the day would come when he would be too weary to rule his kingdom.

'My sons,' he said, 'whoever brings me, in one year's time, the smallest dog shall inherit my kingdom.'

Naturally, the three princes were surprised by this request. But each was desperate to inherit their father's crown, and so all three promised to return with the smallest dog they could find.

The eldest son went north through the mountains. The middle son went south through the desert. But the youngest son rode west, through the deep, dark forest. He rode until he came to a castle with a golden door. Knocking on the door, he watched amazed as it was opened by a pair of floating hands. He followed these hands through the halls and passageways of the castle, and into a vast banqueting hall.

There, three cats played fiddles on a stage, making the most horrendous din, and a crowd of cats sat around a table laid with gold cutlery. The prince was utterly mystified. Shaking his head with wonder, he took an empty seat at the table, beside a small white cat in a silken gown.

'Greetings, my prince,' she said in a beautiful soft voice, 'and welcome to my castle.'

'Thank you, my lady,' said the prince, bowing his head, too befuddled to say more. While his head was bowed, he noticed a portrait on the cat's bracelet. The picture bore a remarkable resemblance to him; it was as though he were gazing into a mirror.

The white cat invited the prince to stay at the castle. She proved a perfect host. In fact, she was so perfect that the prince could not bring himself to leave. Together, they rode and hunted; dined and talked; read and drew and sang. The prince was

The White Cat

blissfully happy and forgot all about his father's kingdom or the quest to find the smallest dog. A whole year passed as in a daze.

But, one morning, the cat sat him down. 'It is only three days until you must return home with the smallest dog,' she reminded him.

The prince smacked his forehead. 'How can I have forgotten such a thing?' he cried, appalled at his absentmindedness. 'Wherever shall I find such a dog in three days?'

'There's no need to worry, my prince,' said the cat. 'I have one here, in my paw.'

And she held out a small acorn.

At first the prince thought the cat mocked him. Then he heard a sound. He bent his ear to the acorn and heard, most distinctly, the bark of a dog.

The prince was taken aback. 'I knew an acorn could come from bark, but I didn't know a bark could come from an acorn!' he exclaimed. 'This is a most peculiar kind of magic!'

Accepting the cat's present, he made a tearful farewell and rode back through the forest to his father's castle. His brothers had also returned. Both carried small dogs, and both looked appallingly smug, confident in their impending victories. When they saw that the youngest prince seemed to have no dog at all, they grew more complacent still.

They showed their tiny dogs to the king. He congratulated them on their efforts.

'And what about you, my son?' said the king, turning to the prince with a frown. 'Have you no dog to show me?'

The Mysterious Cat

Smiling, the youngest prince took the acorn from his pocket and cracked it open. Inside was a miniscule mutt, so tiny it could use a thimble for a basket.

'This is a wonder!' said the king, congratulating his youngest son. 'You have surely won the challenge. However,' he continued, 'I am not yet ready to hand over my kingdom. Whoever returns in a year with a piece of muslin fine enough to pass through the eye of a needle shall have my crown.'

The youngest son rode through the deep, dark forest, back to the castle with the golden door. The prince informed the white cat of the new challenge. She promised to help. But then, as before, he found the castle so peaceful, and the cat's company so pleasant, that days turned to weeks and weeks to months, and he forgot to find the muslin. A whole year drifted past.

'My dearest, there are only three days for you to complete your father's task,' the cat told him one morning.

'Task?' asked the prince, sipping his coffee. 'What task is that?'

'You must return with a piece of muslin fine enough to pass through the eye of a needle,' the cat reminded him.

'Gah!' wailed the prince. 'How did I forget?! Again!'

'Don't worry,' said the cat, 'I can help.' She handed him a walnut. 'Take this gift, my prince, and I promise that you will win the crown.'

The prince returned to his father's castle. His brothers had both found muslin of the finest quality. But when the king tested them, neither of their offerings could fit through the eye of a needle.

The White Cat

'Well, my boy,' said the king, 'let us test *your* offering.'

The youngest son took the cat's walnut from his pocket. But, to his surprise, when he cracked open its shell there was no muslin, just an ordinary nut. The prince was confused. He crushed the walnut and found a hazelnut. Inside the hazelnut was a cherry stone and inside the cherry stone a kernel. He opened the kernel, only to find a grain of wheat. The prince grew flustered. His brothers began to giggle. The king looked furious.

Finally, the prince split the grain with his thumbnail. At first, he thought it empty. Then he spied a tiny strand poking from the wheat. The prince pulled and the strand grew longer. He pulled some more; and he kept pulling until the strand became a piece of fabric hundreds of feet long. The fabric was so extraordinary, and woven from so many gorgeous colours, that the king swore it was a miracle. It passed easily through the eye of a needle.

'My youngest son has surely won this challenge,' said the king. 'However, I am not yet ready to hand over my kingdom. Whoever returns in a year with the fairest bride shall have my crown.'

Once again, the prince rode to the castle with the golden door, and once again he was so happy the year passed as if in a dream.

'There are only three days until you must return home,' said the cat, when the time had come. 'Cut off my head and you shall have the fairest bride.'

'What?! Cut off your head?!' cried the prince, recoiling in horror. 'Are you mad? Why, I love you so much I wouldn't hurt a hair on your little white head!'

'My prince,' urged the cat gently, 'if you love me, trust me: cut off my head.'

The prince, hands shaking and stomach churning, drew his sword. With his eyes tight shut, he swung the blade at the cat's neck.

When he opened his eyes, a princess, the fairest in all the land, stood before him. The other cats had become lords and ladies, and the floating hands had turned into servants. The prince was dumbstruck. He took the princess by the hand and begged her to explain.

The princess told her story. She was the daughter of a king and queen, rulers of six mighty kingdoms. Once, when the princess was very young, the queen had taken a walk through the wild wood. But she had roamed too far and entered the land of the fairies. She found a tumbledown castle, whose enchanted garden bloomed with sumptuous fruit. The fruit looked so beautiful, so tempting, that a fierce longing came over the queen. 'I *must* have that fruit,' she said. But the gates were locked.

She was in despair, when a tiny old woman, haggard and bent, appeared. 'Greetings, my sweet,' croaked the old woman, who was really a wicked fairy. 'My sisters and I will allow you as much fruit as you wish. But only if you hand over your daughter to us.'

'My daughter!' wailed the queen. 'Oh, must it be that?'

But she had been enchanted; she really felt she would die if she didn't eat the fruit. So, desperate, she sent her daughter to live with the old women.

The White Cat

The poor girl was locked inside a tower. There she grew up, unhappy and alone.

One day, many years later, the princess saw a dashing prince at the foot of the tower. Their eyes met, and they fell in love. Within an hour, they had agreed to run away to be married.

Determined to escape, the princess tied her bedsheets into a ladder and began to climb from the window. As she descended, however, she was captured by the fairies. Furious, they grabbed the prince and fed him to their dragon. Then they turned the princess into a white cat and sent her home to her parents. There, she found that all the lords and ladies had transformed into cats and the servants into floating hands.

The only way to break the enchantment, the fairies warned her, was to win the heart of a prince who resembled her first love.

'I look just like the portrait on your bracelet!' exclaimed the prince, when he heard the story. 'And you have my love, heart and soul.' He got down on one knee. 'If you love me too, then we shall be married and rule my father's kingdom.'

The princess did love him, more than all the world, and they set forth to ask the king for his consent.

They arrived at the palace in time for the final test. The two older sons showed their brides. One was blonde, and one was dark, and both were very beautiful. The king could not decide between them.

'What about you?' said the king to his youngest son. 'Have you no bride?'

The Mysterious Cat

'I have nothing but this white cat,' said the prince, for the princess had decided to return to her feline form for the journey.

'A cat?' bellowed the king. 'Is this some kind of joke? What good is a cat?'

But then, with a puff of smoke, the white cat transformed into the princess. The court gasped, for she was truly the fairest of them all. The king agreed that the kingdom now belonged to his youngest son.

'Thank you, your majesty, but we have no need of your kingdom,' said the princess, 'for I have six of my own. I offer one to you and one each to your elder children. That leaves three kingdoms for me and my darling prince – for, with your consent, we are to be married.'

The king gave his consent most heartily, and each of the sons was married, and each had kingdoms to rule. The family lived happily ever after, and happiest of all were the youngest son and his truly remarkable bride.

The Bank Cat

· Australian ·

This story, a nineteenth-century creation, stems from Atha Westbury's book Australian Fairy Tales. *Cats do not feature in Australian folklore before then, and not at all in Aboriginal tales, for the simple reason that cats are not native to the land, being first introduced by Europeans in 1788. Unfortunately, this means they are now classed as an invasive species. And, indeed, their effect on the Australian ecosystem has been disastrous. Native species, unused to the new arrivals, and without the opportunity to evolve suitable defences, have suffered terribly. Cats kill hundreds of millions of creatures each year – including small mammals, birds and reptiles – and are blamed for the extinction of over twenty native species.*

Of course, this has not prevented cats from becoming enormously popular and much loved pets. There are around 5 million pet cats and approximately the same number of feral cats living in Australia.

Once upon a time, on the banks of the Bogan river, there was a little town. There wasn't much there, admittedly – just a pub, a shop, a church and the branch of a small bank – but there it was, nevertheless.

It was a dusty, out-of-the-way place, where nothing of much interest ever happened. Certainly, nothing of much interest had ever happened to young Tony Buck. An orphan, he had been

The Mysterious Cat

taken in by the manager of the bank when he was only a baby. And there he lived, delivering messages and doing odd jobs.

The bank manager was a kind man, but he was also practical: he had no time for stories, or fancies or daydreams. And he had no time for teaching Tony about them either. So, Tony had grown to be a practical young lad, who knew nothing beyond the little town and the little bank; his days were spent delivering messages, sending telegrams and counting money.

One night, Tony was sitting alone in the bank's cramped office, his only company the large fawn-coloured tomcat that had made the bank his home. Tony's boss, the bank manager, was away on business, and he had charged Tony with looking after the place until he returned. But the night was late, and Tony was bored, and he found it harder and harder to keep his eyes open. Time and again, he caught himself nodding off. Each time he jolted awake, he found the cat staring at him.

Now, a more imaginative young lad might have found something odd in the cat's gaze: a curiosity, an intelligence, even a hint of mockery. Tony, however, saw none of that – at least, not at first. But the boy kept fighting off sleep, and the cat kept on staring, and eventually even Tony began to find it disconcerting.

'What are you looking at, furball?' he snapped. 'Can't a chap have a nap by the fire?'

And he closed his eyes once more.

'Who are you calling "furball"?'

Tony, astonished, leapt up with a yelp.

The Bank Cat

'Who's that?' he cried. 'Who spoke?'

'Me, obviously,' said the voice. 'There's no one else here, is there?'

Panicked, Tony looked behind the curtains, and under the table, and through the door. But the place was empty. Slowly, he turned around. His eyes fell upon the cat.

'That's right,' said the cat. 'I said it. And, for the record, I'm not fond of being called "furball". Got that?'

Tony nodded. But for a boy whose days were spent delivering messages, sending telegrams and counting money, this was all a bit much. He flopped back in his chair, rubbing his eyes.

'I—I—I didn't know cats could talk,' he eventually stuttered.

'Well, normally they can't,' admitted the creature.

'But . . . how?'

'No time for explanations,' said the cat, with an impatient wave of his paw. 'Any minute now, the bank will be robbed.'

'Bank? Robbed?' muttered Tony. He couldn't get his head around any of this. But before he had time to ask any more questions, he heard an almighty creak. It was the sound of the bank's front door being tugged off its hinges. This was followed by a thunderous crack – the sound of the door thudding to the floor.

'Cripes! Bank robbers!' gasped Tony. 'What'll I do? The boss is away and I'm all alone!'

The severity of the situation hit him, and the young lad began to cry.

'Stop that nonsense right now!' said the cat. 'Blubbing won't get you anywhere, will it?'

Just then, three men stepped through the empty door. Their clothes were dusty and unkempt, their hats crumpled. On their faces they wore masks; their hands clasped shiny revolvers.

'Bushrangers!' squeaked Tony. 'We're doomed!'

Hearing him, the robbers swivelled. Tony found three guns pointing at him.

'Please!' he wailed. 'Don't shoot!'

'Hold fire, boys,' said the leader of the gang to the others. 'He's just a kid. Listen, lad, we won't shoot if you tell us what we need to know. Now, where is your boss?'

'He's not here!'

'Are you sure? If you're lying, we'll fill you full of holes.'

'I promise! I promise! He's away on business – he won't be back until the morning!'

'Good,' said the bandit. 'In that case, chuck me the keys.'

'But I can't!' snivelled Tony. 'The manager has them!'

'Well, get some other keys then! There must be another set!' insisted the leader.

'No,' sniffed the lad. 'Only the manager is allowed keys.'

The robbers were beyond livid when they heard this. Bundling Tony back into the little office, they tied him to a chair. Then they locked him and the cat inside, while they searched the rest of the bank. Tony could hear them scrabbling through cupboards, flinging open cabinets, rummaging through drawers. There was also the loud *clang-clang-clang* of a hammer on the metal safe. They were trying to force their way in.

The Bank Cat

'Oh dear! Oh no! What am I going to do?' sobbed Tony to himself.

'Honestly!' tutted the cat. 'Will you stop that infernal whinging?'

'But I promised I'd look after the bank. And now I'm all tied up and the bushrangers are robbing it! And there's nothing I can do and there's no one to help me!'

'Why, of course there is!' said the cat, springing onto the chair next to Tony.

'Who?' asked the boy.

'Me, obviously!' said the cat.

Tony looked confused. 'But . . . but how can *you* help me? You're only a cat.'

'Well, yes and no. I didn't used to be a cat, you see.'

'What do you mean? You mean once you were a kitten?'

'No, Tony, I don't mean that at all. I mean that before I was a cat, I was a fairy. One of the cleverest, most powerful of all the fairies in Fairyland, in fact.'

Tony made a little noise, a noise that might have been a disbelieving snort, or a sob of fear, or a whimper of confusion – or perhaps all three.

'You don't believe me, eh?' demanded the cat.

Tony shrugged. But it was clear he didn't, for he had no time for fairies or Fairyland or magic – he had certainly never seen any in his little bank.

'Fine,' sighed the cat. 'I'll prove it then. Say, *Sevle naila rtsua* – but say it very slowly and very clearly.'

The Mysterious Cat

Tony, confused but curious, did as he was told: '*Sevle naila rtsua!*'

Instantly, the cat disappeared. Now, instead, standing on the chair where the cat had been, there was a tiny figure. He was old and thin, but rather dapper, dressed in smart hunting clothes.

'Believe me now?' he laughed.

Tony nodded, mouth agog. 'Who are you?' he managed to ask.

'Weren't you listening? I'm a fairy – a special kind of fairy,' said the little man. 'Remember the words I told you, *Sevle naila rtsua*? Now, say them backwards.'

It took Tony a minute or two but, frowning, he managed to reverse the letters.

'Australian Elves!' he cried. 'It's Australian Elves backwards!'

'That's right,' said the little man. 'I'm one of the Australian Elves, and proud of it.'

'But,' wondered Tony, scratching his head, 'if you're a fairy . . . why were you a cat?'

'Ah, well,' replied the fairy, looking a touch sheepish, 'the other fairies turned me into one.'

'What for?'

'As a punishment. I kept causing too much mischief – even for an elf!' He laughed. 'But luckily for you, I'm good at getting *out* of trouble, as well as into it! So this particular Australian Elf will help you out of this jam.'

He hopped off the chair, and clambered up a filing cabinet to the window, which was open a crack.

The Bank Cat

'Are you leaving me?' asked Tony.

'No, mate, I'm saving you! I'm going to get help!'

And, with that, he crawled through the window and out into the night. Poor Tony was left in the dark, trussed helplessly to the chair. Terrified and alone, he hoped desperately that the fairy would succeed – otherwise the bank would be robbed, and he'd be at the mercy of those ruffians. Tony shuddered.

All this while, the robbers had been ransacking the bank, and all the time the *clang-clang-clang* of the hammer on the safe had been echoing around the building. Now, Tony heard the men cry out with delight. They had broken through the door.

'We're in!'

'That's it, boys!'

'We're rich! Rich!'

But, before the gang had time to make off with the money, let alone spend it, the police arrived. They burst into the bank, taking the robbers completely by surprise. In a matter of moments, the bushrangers were disarmed and handcuffed. And, from there, the rascals were flung in jail, where they spent a very long, very uncomfortable couple of years.

As the thieves were dragged away, kicking and cursing, Tony noticed a movement by the window. It was the tiny man. With a doff of his hat, he winked a wink and grinned a grin. Then, just like that, he disappeared, never to be seen again.

The bank manager, when he returned, was astounded to learn of the events that had taken place in his absence – or, at least, *nearly* all the events. Young Tony kept the part about the

Australian Elf to himself; he knew the practical bank manager would never believe him.

So, the bank manager was relieved to learn that Tony was unharmed. He was even more relieved to learn that his money was safe.

But, ever afterwards, one matter nagged at him. Where on earth had his cat got to?

Johnny Reed's Cat

· English ·

The following story is a variation on 'The King of the Cats', a mainstay of British folklore. The earliest known version of 'The King of the Cats' is 'Beware the Cat' by author and printer William Baldwin, published in 1561. There are, though, endless interpretations from throughout the British Isles. Most commonly, these tales end with the cat revealing itself to be the king – before disappearing, never to be seen again. However, in this version – an old folk tale from the Newcastle area – the cat is not the monarch, but a lovelorn and grief-stricken tom.

Perhaps the reason the story is so pervasive, and so persistent, is that it reflects several truths about cats: the way they act with a regal haughtiness, an effortless superiority, that suggests they know they are of royal birth. And the fact that it feels as if cats can understand us, and could reply any time they wished, if only our human speech were not so beneath them.

Johnny Reed dug graves for the local churchyard. He and his wife had no children, but they had a cat, and this moggy was a great comfort, for Johnny's job was hard for body and soul.

One dark night Johnny hurried home from the graveyard, the winter wind nipping at his nose. He was dreaming of his nice warm fire and his nice warm slippers, when he discovered a most uncanny scene.

The Mysterious Cat

By the road, a cluster of shadows and lights twirled and whirled in peculiar patterns.

'What's this now?' thought Johnny, going to investigate. As he inched closer, the lights grew brighter, and the shadows darker, until even Johnny – who was not faint-hearted – began to tremble in his boots.

'Could it be ghosts and ghouls?' he fretted. 'Or perhaps it's a coven of witches, up to no good?'

But presently he was close enough to see that it was none of those things.

Nine cats danced in a circle. Their fur, black as midnight, had been the twirling shadows; their eyes glistening in the moonlight the whirling lights. They were dancing a merry jig, paw in paw. The sight sent a chill down Johnny's spine.

'It ain't natural!' he thought. 'Cats dancing like people! Whatever next!'

So, he shouted and stamped, trying to scare away the creatures. But they continued dancing, as if he were no more bother than a butterfly.

'Johnny Reed!' a voice called from the darkness.

'Who's that?' said Johnny. He spun around, but he could see no other person.

'Johnny Reed!' the voice called once more.

'I'm here!' Johnny shouted angrily. 'Show yourself!'

'Johnny Reed! Look down! It was I who spoke to you,' said the voice. And the largest of the cats stepped from the dance.

Well, that was the final straw for Johnny. He'd had a cat

scratch him, and he'd had a cat lick him, but he'd never had a cat call him by his name.

'If he can talk, who knows what else he can do?' Johnny thought to himself. 'He might have all kinds of peculiar magic! I better be polite to the creature or else he'll turn me into a toad!'

So, doffing his cap to the cat, he said, 'How can I be of service, sir?'

'You can tell Dan that his Peggy is dead,' replied the cat. Then it danced into the darkness of the night, vanishing with all its fellows.

Johnny ran home feeling bothered and bewildered. He thought of every person he knew, but he couldn't recollect a single person called Dan. And if he didn't know Dan, how could he deliver the cat's message?

Crashing through the door with such a clatter his wife jumped with fright, he slumped down in his chair by the fire.

'Dan? Who's Dan?' he begged his wife. 'I need to find Dan!'

'Dan? There's no one named Dan round here,' she said. 'Why do you ask?'

'Because I need to tell Dan that his Peggy is dead.'

At this, Johnny's cat, who had been dozing by the fire, sprang up.

'What?! Can it be?' he cried. 'My dear Peggy is dead! Alas, alack!'

And without further ado, the cat fled the house and was never seen again.

Kisa the Cat

· Icelandic ·

Cats are believed to have arrived in Scandinavia during the Viking Age, possibly brought back by a raiding party. They soon became widespread, being kept not only on land, but also on ships, where they were used for pest control. Sadly, there's also evidence they were farmed for their fur, a protection against the chilly northern winters.

As in most cultures, cats soon found a place in folklore and myth. In one Norse tale, Thor was challenged to lift a house cat. Despite being the strongest of the gods, Thor failed to pull the animal from the floor; it twisted and stretched, but its paws never left the ground. The god had, however, been fooled by an illusion: the cat was none other than Jörmungandr, the Midgard Serpent, whose monstrous form coiled around the world.

Cats were also closely associated with Freyja, the goddess of love, war and fertility, who rode in a flying chariot pulled by two grey tomcats, Bygul and Trjegul. Because of this, Freyja rewarded with good fortune those who showed kindness and respect to cats – and punished those who did not.

The following Icelandic fairy tale was introduced to English-speaking readers when it featured in The Brown Fairy Book *by Andrew Lang – itself an adaptation of a version in Adeline Rittershaus's* Neuisländischen Volksmärchen.

Kisa the Cat

Once upon a time there was a queen with a beautiful grey cat. It was a playful animal, and the queen was fonder of it than she was of any human being. One spring, the cat had a kitten. From then on, the cat spent all her time with her child and was too busy to play with the queen. The woman's heart ached. Not only had she lost her dearest friend, but she was horribly jealous, for she longed for a child of her own.

Entering the bedchamber one day, the cat found the queen crying on her bed.

'Why do you weep, your majesty?' she asked.

'Because you are so happy with your kitten,' said the queen, 'while I have no child to hold and no cat to cuddle.'

Pained to see the queen so sad, the cat asked a fairy to bless the woman with a baby. Nine months later, the queen had a daughter – a darling child, as sparkling and radiant as sunlight on snow.

As the princess grew, her favourite playmate was the cat's kitten, Kisa. The child adored the kitten. She would not fall asleep without it curled up by her feet.

One bedtime, however, the kitten was nowhere to be found. There was a tremendous fuss. The servants searched the palace up and down – in the ballroom and the great hall; in the kitchens and the larder; in the library and the tower and the moat and the dungeon – but Kisa had vanished.

Time ticked on, and eventually the young princess forgot the kitten. She learned to walk and talk. She learned to read and write. But most of all she learned to play, for she was an adventurous child who loved to roam the palace grounds. One day, in the course of her exploring, she stumbled upon an overgrown corner of the garden. There she found a tiny blue-grey cat.

'Good morning, princess,' said the cat, nuzzling the child's leg. 'Do you remember me?'

The princess shook her head, for she had been a baby the last time they'd met.

'I'm Kisa,' the cat continued. 'I'm your foster sister.'

'But I don't have a sister!' laughed the princess. 'And, anyway, you can't be my sister; you're a cat.'

'Well, I slept in your cot every night for a year,' explained Kisa, 'and you never once fell asleep without me to warm you.'

'How lovely!' smiled the girl.

Just then, a pair of servants blundered through the undergrowth, calling the child's name. Kisa, startled, disappeared into the trees.

The next morning, the princess decided to explore the forest. It was a hot summer's day, and the girl felt light and free as she skipped down the pebbly path by the river. Birds sang and bees buzzed; the sun glinted and glimmered on the water. Lost in her daydreams, the young princess meandered smack into a giant. He was a massive, hulking creature with legs as thick as fir trees and skin as rough as bark.

'Now then, what have we here?' growled the giant, peering down at the princess. 'A little-bitty human? Oh good!' He patted his tummy. 'I haven't eaten one of them for ages!'

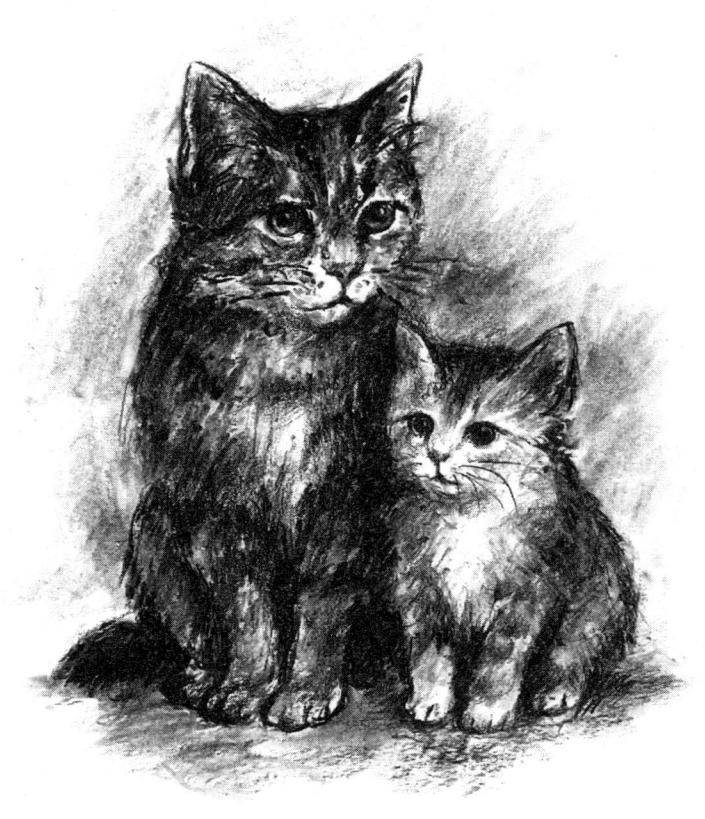

And he reached down and plucked the girl up in his humungous fist.

Tying a vine around the girl's waist, he dragged her down the path towards his cave. But the princess kicked and screamed and argued and bawled, and made such a frightful racket, that soon the giant regretted kidnapping her in the first place.

'Stop your yapping!' he snapped, kneading his brow. 'You're giving me a headache!'

Wanting to rest his eyes, he sat down and leant his back against a boulder. Before falling into a deep slumber, however, he lopped off the princess's feet to prevent her from running away.

'Oh, help!' cried the princess, trying to be heard above the giant's snores. 'Help me someone, please!'

Before long, there came the rattle of wooden wheels. A cart hurtled through the trees. Kisa jumped from the vehicle, helped the princess onto the back, and raced through the forest to her hut.

The princess had escaped the giant. She was, though, still in the most awful pain. Kisa gave her warm milk to drink and licked at the wounds where the girl's feet had been. Gradually, the pain eased, and the princess drifted off to sleep, snoring nearly as thunderously as the giant.

Kisa, meanwhile, went to find the giant. He was in his cave, eating soup with his wife.

'When I catch her, I'm going kill that noisy princess,' grumbled the brute, 'and bake her in a casserole.'

'Dear oh dear! What a silly thing to say!' tutted his wife.

'You know little girls don't make good casseroles. She'd be so much tastier in a nice stew.'

'I don't care, just so long as she's dead!' said the giant gruffly.

'Well, you should never have let her escape,' said his wife. 'It was awfully careless of you.'

'You think I don't know that?' protested the giant. He jabbed his thumb at the princess's bloody feet, which he'd tossed in a corner. 'I should have cut off her head instead of her feet.'

While they plotted and griped, Kisa crept to the cooking pot and tipped a great sack of salt into the soup. As the giants slurped, they grew thirstier and thirstier. Eventually, their throats grew so parched they stomped down to the river for a drink.

While they were gone, the cat grabbed the princess's feet and made her way back to the hut. With a few strands of magic grass, she bound the feet to the princess's bloody stumps. After a minute or two, the little princess was whole again. It was another week, however, before she was well enough to return to the palace.

The king and queen, meanwhile, had been sick with worry over their missing daughter. They were overjoyed when Kisa brought her home. Once they heard the story of the giant, they hugged the cat most tenderly, declaring her their greatest friend.

'However can we thank you, dear Kisa?' they gushed. 'Name a reward – anything, anything at all – and you shall have it.'

The cat shook her head. 'Perhaps one day I'll claim my reward,' she said. 'But not today.' And she slipped once more into the trees.

Years passed, as they must, even for princesses. Her childhood ended, and it was time to find a husband. The king and queen invited every prince from every land to the palace, but none of them was worthy of the princess. Some were too boastful or too vain; others were too boring or too stupid.

But, finally, a prince arrived who was the princess's equal. Like her, he was intelligent and witty, more interested in woods than wine and preferring books to ballrooms. They married. The king and queen threw the grandest feast the kingdom had ever known. And among the hundreds of guests was Kisa.

The princess shed tears of joy when they met.

'Darling Kisa, have you come to claim your reward?' she said, clasping her friend's paw.

'Yes, princess.'

'Oh, lovely! Would you like a golden tiara? A box of jewels? Or a small island, perhaps?'

'No, none of those things,' said the cat. 'I would like to spend the night at the foot of your bed, as I did when we were children.'

'Is that all?' said the princess, wrinkling her nose. She was disappointed to be asked for such a puny gift. She would have gladly handed over a pile of gold and silver. But the cat insisted: she wanted to spend the night on the princess's bed, nothing more nor less.

'Well, if that's what you want, then that's what you shall have,' said the princess.

So, that night, the princess fell asleep with Kisa purring softly at her feet.

Kisa the Cat

In the morning, however, when the princess awoke, she found the cat transformed into a woman. After much confusion and excitement, Kisa told her tale.

Kisa's mother had been human. She had fallen foul of an evil fairy, who, jealous of the woman's beauty, had placed a curse upon her: unless she performed a truly heroic deed, she was condemned to spend her life as a cat. She died before she had a chance to complete such an act. The enchantment continued with her daughter, Kisa. In rescuing the princess, however, Kisa had performed a truly heroic act – finally bringing the curse to an end.

Kisa lived at the princess's court for several years. She was every bit as beautiful and kind as a human as she had been as a cat. And so, I imagine, Kisa married a handsome young prince and went to live in a castle, for such is the fate of beautiful princesses.

The Poor Miller's Boy and the Cat

· German ·

This story belongs to perhaps the most celebrated of all story collections, Grimms' Fairy Tales. First published in 1812, it is a masterpiece of both literature and folklore, and contains some of the greatest, most celebrated stories ever told, including 'Little Red Riding Hood', 'Rapunzel' and 'Hansel and Gretel'.

Cats features in a number of the tales and they did much to rehabilitate the cat in German culture. Since medieval times, cats had been tarred with the same brush as elsewhere in Europe: witchcraft, devilry and black magic. When the Brothers Grimm compiled their great treasury, however, a different cat emerged: still supernatural, but no longer diabolical. In this tale, the cat is capable of great magic but, far from being devilish, she is mysterious and enchanting. It is an example of a tale type known as the 'Animal Bride', in which a prince falls in love with a talking animal, who is later revealed to be a beautiful princess.

Once upon a time there lived an old miller. He had never been blessed with a wife or child and his only family were his three apprentices. The miller grew older and frailer by the day, until his knees creaked and his back ached, and he longed to sleep by the fire.

The Poor Miller's Boy and the Cat

'It is nearly time for me to retire,' he told the three apprentices. 'Go out into the world; whoever finds me the finest horse shall have the mill.'

The three apprentices left the next morning and journeyed until it was time to make camp for the night. They found a cave and there they curled up, as if to go to sleep.

However, the two older boys decided to play a trick on the third lad, Hans. He was often the butt of their jokes. Hans was always daydreaming when he should have been working, and laughing when he should have been serious, so they thought him a fool. Waiting until they heard his snores, the two boys tiptoed from the cave and out into the dark night.

Hans woke to find himself all alone. He was dreadfully afraid, and when he left the cave and found himself in a gloomy forest, he was even more frightened, for he didn't know which way to go.

'I'll never find a horse now,' he thought mournfully. Lost and alone, he wandered hither and thither, kicking a pebble along the path.

'Where are you going, Hans?' said a voice. Puzzled, the lad looked around. All he could see was a small cinnamon-coloured cat, dainty and elegant.

'I—I don't know,' stammered Hans, confused to be talking to a cat.

'Let me help you, Hans,' said the cat.

'You can't help me,' said Hans glumly. 'No one can.'

The Mysterious Cat

'I *can* help you – and I will,' said the cat. 'But first you must be my loyal servant for seven years. Then I will find you the finest horse in all the world.'

Promising to serve her for seven years, Hans went to live in the cat's fabulous castle. It was packed with cats: cat butlers and cat cooks, cat housemaids and cat cleaners.

That evening there was a tremendous feast. Plate after plate of delicious food was laid before Hans. He had never eaten so much or so well. After he was too full to swallow another mouthful, the cat invited him to dance.

'I'm sorry,' said Hans, shaking his head. 'I couldn't dance with a cat. It wouldn't feel right.'

The next morning, he was woken by the cat's servants, who washed and dressed him, and treated him like a prince. And then he was handed a silver axe and sent to chop wood.

Years passed, flying by as if they were weeks. Hans was feasted and indulged, and in return he chopped wood with his silver axe and mowed the meadow with a golden scythe. Then, one day, the cat asked him to build her a house. Hans built a small cottage with wooden beams and a thatched roof, and very pretty it was too. The cat seemed pleased.

'You have now served me for seven years, as you promised,' she said. 'In return, I will fulfil my vow to you. Go to the stables, Hans, and look at the horses.'

In the stables Hans found twelve horses, magnificent beyond his imaginings. But which, he wondered, was the finest? Finally, after much humming and hawing, he selected a beautiful bay with white feet and a lustrous mane – for, truly, he had never seen a more handsome creature in all his days. But when he tried to lead the horse outside, the cat stopped him, saying, 'Not yet, Hans, not yet. Go home to the mill and I will bring you the horse in three days' time.'

When Hans returned to the mill he found the other apprentices waiting. They took one look at him and chortled, for in all Hans' years with the cat he had never received a new coat or a new pair of boots. Dusty from his long journey, he was ragged and filthy. They laughed again when they realised that he had brought no horse.

'Where's your horse, Hans?' they jeered. 'Did you forget to bring one?'

Hans ignored their taunts. 'My horse will be here tomorrow,' he said politely. And his rivals laughed a third time, believing Hans to be as big a fool as ever.

The miller, too, had no warm welcome for Hans. He was appalled by Hans' tattered clothes and grimy face and wouldn't allow him to eat at the dinner table or to sleep in a bed. Instead, the lad was bundled into the yard and thrown a chunk of bread. Damp and miserable, he fell asleep in the old goose house.

The next morning, Hans woke to the rumble of wheels and the clatter of hooves. He rushed to the goose-house window. Three days had passed, and the cat had arrived in a golden coach, pulled by six fine horses. But when the coach door opened, Hans had a tremendous surprise. For stepping from the carriage was no small cinnamon cat; it was a woman. Hans' mistress had transformed into a beautiful princess.

'Where is Hans?' she asked.

'Hans?' said the flummoxed miller. 'Why, he's in the goose house! The lad's a disgrace! He wasn't fit to spend the night under my roof.'

Hans, dazed and only half awake, was fetched by the princess's servants. They scrubbed his face and brushed his hair and dressed him in the richest silks. As if by magic, the ragged miller's boy vanished. In his place was a fine-looking fellow, fit for any royal court.

'It is time to judge which of your apprentices has the best horse,' the princess told the miller.

The first apprentice brought his horse, and though it was tall and powerful, it was as blind as a mole. The second apprentice brought his horse, and though its coat was glossy, its hind leg was as crooked as a church spire. And then a third horse – Hans' horse – was brought into the yard. Its coat shone, its eyes sparkled, its bearing was proud and noble. The horse was, without any doubt, the finest in all the world.

The miller had to admit he had never seen a better horse. 'The mill shall go to Hans,' he conceded through gritted teeth.

But the princess told the miller to keep his mill, for Hans had no need of it. She and Hans returned in the golden coach to the spot where Hans had built a house. But instead of a small cottage with a thatched roof, there was now a wondrous castle, with turrets and towers. And the interior was equally spectacular, for there was scarcely an object not made of gold or silver or studded with gems and diamonds.

The princess, who had once been a cat, married Hans, the miller's boy, and the two of them were content for the rest of their days. The miller and his two apprentices, meanwhile, learned a valuable lesson: those who seem odd or different are often the happiest in the end.

The Boy Who Drew Cats

· Japanese ·

Cats have been widespread in Japan since the twelfth century. Since that time, they have featured prominently in the nation's folklore, often as Kaibyō, *or 'strange cats'.*

The most infamous of these supernatural cats are the bakeneko. *Born ordinary pet cats, they undergo a transformation after being excessively long-lived, becoming malicious spirits capable of morphing into humans. They may even kill their own masters, steal their appearance and replace them. These shapeshifters possess other magical abilities, including speaking human languages, being superb dancers, eating impossible amounts of food and placing curses on people.*

Bakeneko are a form of yōkai, *or supernatural being. Other cat* yōkai *include:* kasha, *corpse-stealing cat demons;* nekomusume, *a cat–human hybrid resembling a person but incapable of speech; and the human-hunting* nekomata, *a giant two-tailed cat.*

Despite these terrifying felines, cats are symbols of good fortune in Japan. The cats in this story – an old tale with roots in a fifteenth-century legend – have qualities from both sides of the Japanese cat, therefore: they are bringers of good luck but also powerful, violent forces of the supernatural.

The Boy Who Drew Cats

Many years ago, in a village in Japan, there lived a sickly child. Deciding he would never be strong enough to work on the farm, his parents packed him off to be a priest.

At the temple he was trained by an old man. But though the boy was bright, the priest worried he would fail his training, for the boy had one very singular quirk: he loved to draw cats. In fact, he couldn't stop drawing cats. He drew them in his books, and in the dust on the floor, and on his arms, and on the walls, and on the pillars and, well, everywhere.

The priest explained, not unkindly, that a good student should spend his time studying, not drawing pictures of cats. So, the boy tried to break the habit. He did his best to concentrate on his lessons. But, all the while, cats drifted through his mind, meowing and mewling, pleading to be drawn.

After a day or two, he could contain them no longer. The pictures came pouring out: black cats, white cats and tabby cats; drowsy cats, running cats and laughing cats; jumping cats, juggling cats and fighting cats.

The priest was disappointed. 'You are no more a priest than you are a farmer,' he said sadly. 'I'm sorry, you must leave the temple. But remember this: stay away from large spaces and stick to the small.'

Well, the boy had no idea what the priest's words meant. But he had no choice but to leave the temple. He packed his bag and left.

Confused and worried, the boy wandered aimlessly down the road. He felt lost and utterly alone. He couldn't stay at the temple, for he was no longer welcome; he couldn't return home, for his parents would be furious; and he couldn't look for work, for he was too sickly and fragile.

Not knowing what to do, the boy kept walking. As night fell, he reached the next village. All was dark but for one light winking in the window of a large temple.

'Perhaps they will train me there,' thought the boy. 'Or at least give me shelter for the night.'

Unbeknownst to the boy, however, the temple had long been abandoned. Years before, it had been invaded by a goblin. The creature destroyed the temple and chased away the priests. The light in the window was not a sign of welcome; it was a trap to lure travellers to their doom.

The boy rang the bell. No one came. He rang again. No answer. By now, however, the boy was cold and hungry and terribly tired; he longed for a bite to eat and a nice warm place to sleep. So, slowly, he pushed open the door.

'Hello?' the boy called. 'Hello?' But there was no reply except his echo.

Gingerly, he stepped into the dark, ghostly temple. Great strings of cobwebs hung from the pillars. Dust lay on the floor, thick as a carpet. Everywhere he looked he saw decay and ruin: broken pillars, collapsed ceilings, ripped up floorboards.

'Oh dear,' thought the boy, realising there was to be no warm welcome. 'But perhaps I should still look for some food. And sweep these cobwebs. And find a bed for the night.'

But the boy did none of these things. He didn't look for food, or sweep the cobwebs, or find a bed for the night.

Instead, he drew cats. He drew cat after cat after cat. He drew on the walls, and the columns, and the floor. He drew on the mats, and the screens, and the statues. He drew on the dust, and the rubble, and the cobwebs.

Eventually, however, his hand cramped and his eyes grew heavy. Yawning, the boy searched for a place to rest his head. But everywhere was too large and cold. Suddenly, with a shudder, he remembered the words of the old priest: 'Stay away from large spaces and stick to the small.'

That made the boy pause. 'Hmm. This room is certainly large,' he thought nervously. 'Perhaps I should find somewhere smaller.' So, instead of sleeping in the great hall, he decided to bed down in a little cupboard in the corner. Exhausted, he fell asleep immediately.

His rest did not last long. Around midnight, he was woken by bloodcurdling noises: screams and cries; bangs and bumps; rattles and crashes and thuds. The boy was terrified. He huddled in his cupboard, waiting for the sun to rise.

In the morning, when he felt the coast was clear, he inched from his hidey-hole. There, in a pool of blood on the temple floor, lay a monstrous goblin. A giant scaly rat, as big as a horse, it had enormous claws and flesh-tearing teeth. Its hairless tail ended in a ragged mess, the tip torn off.

The boy, appalled, prodded the creature with his toe, checking it was dead.

'I wonder who killed it?' he thought, for the place seemed deserted. He glanced around; and, as he did so, his attention was drawn to his pictures. To his shock, he saw that the drawings had changed. Instead of laughing or yawning or playing, the cats now were fierce, their teeth stained with blood. One, a tiny tabby, had something dangling from its jaws.

'Why, it's the tip of the goblin's tail!' the boy said. 'How on earth did that happen?'

The boy was baffled. He did not know how or why, but the cats – his cats – had killed the goblin and freed the temple.

Once news of the monster's death became known, the priests returned, and the villagers threw a feast. The boy's hand was shaken so many times he feared it would fall off.

His fame spread far and wide, for he was an artist so talented his drawings could strike down goblins. Soon, the young man was renowned throughout the land. But no matter where he went or who he met, he only ever drew one thing: pictures of cats.

The Enchanted Cat

· Hungarian ·

This Hungarian story has everything you could possibly hope for from a fairy tale: princes, palaces, sorcerers, black magic, betrayal, intrigue, evil stepmothers – and, of course, a cat who saves the day.

It was first collected and translated into English in 1895 by Baroness Orczy (author of The Scarlet Pimpernel*). But its roots are much older and lost to time. As Orczy herself said, it would take 'two score or more Eastern and Western, Latin, Teutonic or Slavonic languages' to trace its origins. That, however, did not stop it becoming a much loved tale – for, Orczy wrote, 'in their earliest childhoods Hungarian children' heard of the doings of the wicked queen and the enchanted cat.*

Incidentally, cats are enormously popular in Hungary, with the country having the highest per-capita cat ownership in the EU. There is even a museum dedicated to them in Budapest.

Once upon a time, in a faraway land, a beloved queen died. Her death left a prince without a mother and a king without a wife. Though the king was heartbroken, he knew his kingdom required a queen. So, a year and a day later, he remarried, taking a beautiful widow with a young son for his bride. However, the new queen, though a rare beauty, possessed a cold and wicked heart. She had no love for the king or his kingdom; she cared only for wealth and power – and for her own son, who she hoped one day would wear the crown.

Time passed, and the king grew ill. Too weak to perform his duties, he decided the prince should rule. The king made an announcement: in three days' time his son would marry and inherit the kingdom.

The queen fumed at the news. She had always planned to kill the prince and place *her* son on the throne. But now her plans were in tatters. Once crowned, she knew, the prince would be so well guarded it would be nigh on impossible to harm him.

So, that night, under the cover of darkness, the queen visited the home of a powerful sorcerer. In a hushed voice, she asked him to murder the prince. But the sorcerer refused.

'Magic cannot take a life, your majesty,' he explained. 'However, I have in my possession a potion. One drop on the prince's body will transform him into a black cat. You can kill the cat, and no one will be the wiser.'

The sorcerer took a bottle of potion from a shelf and poured a measure into a vial. As he handed it to the queen, he offered her a warning: 'Your majesty, the spell does not last forever. On the night of the new moon the magic will fail, and the prince will regain his true form.'

With the vial hidden on her, the queen crept back through the palace, past the snoring guards, to the door of the prince's bedroom. She dared not enter the young man's room itself. Instead, she sprinkled a few drops of poison on the floor. She knew that the barefooted prince would tread in the mixture on his way to breakfast.

The next morning, the prince had vanished. The palace and its grounds were searched – and then the town, and then the whole kingdom – but the young man could not be found.

The king's heart was broken once more. He had lost his darling first wife, and now, in his old age, he had lost his son and heir. His only comfort was the arrival, that very morning, of a fine black cat. Stroking this affectionate creature seemed to ease his sorrow. Immediately, the grief-stricken old man and the handsome moggy became inseparable.

The situation infuriated the queen. She ached to kill the cat, knowing it to be the prince.

'I *must* kill the creature!' she thought. 'And I must do it soon: I have only ten days until the new moon, when the sorcerer's magic will wear off!'

But the days ticked by and, for all her efforts, she never had the chance to strike, for the king never let the animal out of his sight. During the day, the cat purred on the king's lap; and at night, it curled up at the foot of his bed.

Finally, with only two days left, the queen slipped a sleeping potion into her husband's cocoa. With the king snoring soundly, she bundled the cat into a sack. Then she tossed the sack out the window into the lake.

'That's the end of *him*!' thought the queen. 'And good riddance too!'

But the next morning, who should be sunning itself on the terrace but the cat! The prince's fiancée had seen the cat drop from the sky and splash into the water and had sent her attendants to rescue the poor creature.

The queen was furious. 'Tonight is the new moon,' she seethed, 'when the sorcerer's magic will wear off. This is my last chance to kill that blasted cat!'

She ordered her son to catch a fish. They left the fish on the terrace with a piece of string tied around its tail. Before long, the cat padded up, delighted to have found a juicy meal. But when he went to take a bite, the queen's son pulled on the string, and the fish shot backwards. The cat tried again; and, again, the fish slid back. Then, just as the cat was about to make a third attempt, the queen's son grabbed him. The cat was carried, slashing and biting, towards the lake.

'I'm going to drown you, you useless fluff ball,' hissed the queen's son, 'and then *I'll* be king.'

But, at the moment the cat's head was plunged in the water, the new moon peeked out from behind a cloud. Instantly, the sorcerer's magic wore off. The cat became a human prince once more. And he was a very angry human prince, for his stepbrother was trying to drown him. They fought in the lake, punching and dunking, kicking and splashing. Eventually, the prince managed to drag the queen's son to the shore and take him prisoner.

The queen, however, escaped and was never seen again.

Nevertheless, her evil ways had been found out. The king banished both the queen and her son from the kingdom. Then the prince married his fiancée, succeeded his father as king, and lived happily for the rest of his days.

3

The Mischievous Cat

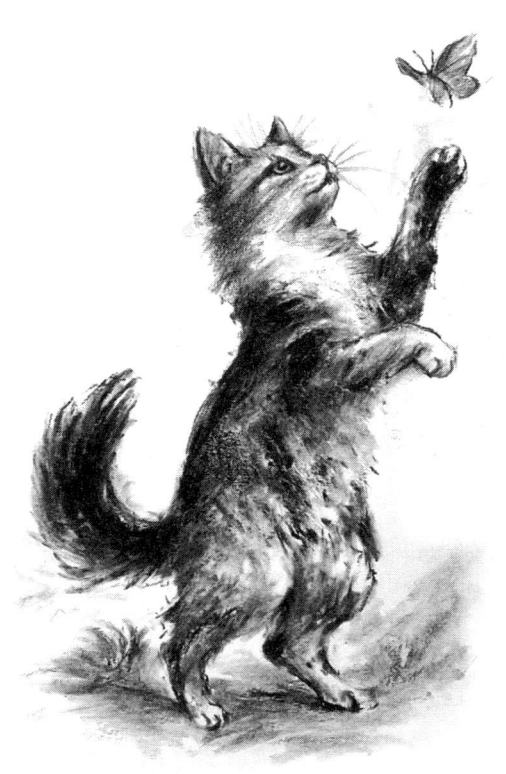

Cats cannot be trusted.

Cats will pilfer your smoked salmon. They will wake sleeping babies. They will trip elderly relatives. Cats will pull over Christmas trees, unwrap birthday presents, and trample muddy pawprints on new blankets. Cats will lurk on the staircase in the dark. They will dash between legs. They will leap on your shoulder when you're holding hot tea. Cats will knock vases off mantelpieces, wipe fresh paint on their tails, and sit in sparkly glue. Cats will scratch sofas, gatecrash online meetings, and send emails with their bottoms.

If you close a door, they will try to open it. If you make a meal, they will try to eat it. If you hide something, they will try to find it. They will go missing at the most inconvenient moments, and turn up at the most inopportune times. They will squeeze into places they are not allowed, and out of places they should be. They are impish tricksters, evil geniuses, and charming anti-heroes – all at once. They will, essentially, do whatever they want, however they fancy, whenever they please – regardless of rules, or safety, or common sense.

In short, cats are troublemakers.

And it can be hard not to take it personally. They are, you feel, doing this deliberately.

This mischievous side explains why cats often feature as tricksters in fairy tales. A stock character throughout world literature, tricksters are quick-witted, rule-breaking rascals. Morally ambiguous, they skate the boundary between good and bad: now using their guile for noble ends, now for evil, and now simply for their own strange amusement. Roguishly charming, they are witty and entertaining, but not to be trusted.

The trickery of cats can be endearing, cunning, frustrating and not always completely harmless. Sometimes their 'mischievous' behaviour is prompted by boredom, at others curiosity or determination. Cats can be remarkably intelligent and can learn new behaviours. So high are their observational and problem-solving skills, estimates suggest that a fully grown cat's IQ is equivalent to a child of two or three. Indeed, cats can be successfully trained. In the 1820s, Signor Capelli staged a show, billed as 'the greatest wonder in England', in which a band of cats performed a musical act, banging drums and ringing bells. In the late nineteenth century, meanwhile, George Techow's Wonderful Performing Cats toured vaudeville theatres, jumping through hoops of fire, walking on their front paws, and dancing along tightropes.

Of course, most cats are not so highly skilled (or so obedient). But that does not prove them unintelligent. Proud and self-sufficient, they simply fail to see why they should be bossed around. After all, cats believe that they are the ones in charge; that they should be giving the orders. They soon learn that certain behaviours – mewling, scratching doors, grabbing legs – elicit certain responses. If they are annoying enough, they think, we may do what they want. And they are usually right.

By watching and imitating, they acquire all manner of behaviours and tricks: turning off lights, opening boxes, opening doors. This intelligence is used mainly to achieve their own felonious ends: pinching food or ferreting out entrances and exits. But they are not entirely selfish. Plenty of documented examples exist of cats engaging their quick wits to help others: cats fetching aid for sick owners, waking families to save them from fires, attacking those who threaten their loved ones.

So, in real cats, as in the cats in these tales, mischievousness and intelligence come in many varieties: from heroic to villainous, from triumphant to fruitless, from playful to deadly. Puss in Boots is the best known of cat tricksters. Wickedly smart, he is ever ready with a new scheme or a glib lie. But all his machinations are for the benefit of his friend, and all are performed with such puckish panache that he is inevitably forgiven by the reader. In other tales, the cat is conniving, usually in the hope of deceiving its prey, or perhaps outfoxing an enemy.

Much like these characters, cats keep their owners permanently on their toes. No matter how much you love your cat, you cannot trust them an inch. They are constantly dipping into their bag of tricks to stage Houdini-like escapes or pull off baffling and brilliant thefts. We sigh and we tut and we shake our heads in frustration – only to forgive them a heartbeat later. It is, after all, impossible to stay angry at a cat. Because however rascally and untrustworthy and manipulative they are, we would not want them any other way.

Puss in Boots

· European ·

The roots of 'Puss in Boots' stretch back to at least 1550, when it was included (as 'Costantino and His Cat') in the Italian writer Giovanni Francesco Straparola's The Facetious Nights of Straparola. *The story also bears similarities to a number of other tales, including 'Lord Peter' (Scandinavian), 'Count Martin of the Cat' (Italian), and 'Domingo's Cat' (Brazilian).*

Its most famous telling, however, remains in Charles Perrault's Stories or Tales from Past Times, with Morals – *nowadays more simply known as* Perrault's Fairy Tales. *This seminal work, published in French in 1697, was one of the earliest and most influential collections of literary fairy tales, featuring such classics as 'Cinderella' and 'Sleeping Beauty'.*

'Puss in Boots', though, is the equal of any of these. One of the great Animal as Helper stories, its cat hero is charming, charismatic and enjoyably crafty. Rightfully, it has gone on to be told and retold countless times, and features in operas, films, picture books, novels and pantomimes.

Once upon a time there lived a miller with three sons. When he died his worldly goods were divided between them. The eldest son was left the mill. The middle son was left the mule. But the youngest son was left only the cat – and very unhappy he was, too.

'My eldest brother will grow rich from the mill,' he sulked. 'And the owner of a mule can always make a living. But all I have is one poxy cat, and when I eat that, I'll have nothing at all.'

Puss was no ordinary cat, however. He was a magnificent, long-furred tabby – very striking and rather vain. He loved to cut a dash, and always wore a splendid hat, cocked at a jaunty angle: black, wide-brimmed, with a plume of red feathers bursting from the band. With a great show of gallantry, Puss would sweep off this hat whenever he met a lady, whether she be a queen or a maid. What's more, Puss – a charming, cunning creature – possessed the gift of the gab.

'Master,' he said, when he overheard his new owner's plan, 'eating me won't do you much good. You'd do better to buy me a pouch and a pair of boots – then I'll prove you got a better gift than either of your brothers.'

The young man was astonished to hear the cat speak. 'Any animal that can talk is worth listening to,' he thought, and he bought Puss the boots and pouch.

Looking very dapper in his shiny new shoes, Puss filled the pouch with carrots and went to hunt for rabbits. But he didn't take a gun or a bow or even a metal trap. He simply stretched out on his back in a field and waited. Sure enough, not fifteen minutes had gone by before a young rabbit stuck its head into the pouch. Then – whoosh! – the cat pulled the pouch strings tight, killing the rabbit stone dead.

Puss took the rabbit to the royal palace, where he was granted an interview with the king.

Puss bowed flamboyantly, with a flourish of his hat. 'Your majesty,' he said, 'allow me to present a gift from my master, the noble Marquess of Carabas.'

And he handed the king the rabbit. There was, in fact, no such person as the Marquess of Carabas, for the cat had invented him. But kings enjoy presents as much as the rest of us and he was thrilled with his gift.

'I thank your master, the noble Marquess of Carabas, and send him my compliments,' the king said.

Over the following months, Puss presented the king with many gifts. Each was offered in the name of the Marquess of Carabas who, though he was yet to meet him, the king had come to consider a very dear friend.

Then one day Puss heard of a trip the king planned to take with his daughter.

'Master, do as I say,' he said to the miller's son, 'and all our troubles will be over. Tomorrow morning, bathe in the river between the bridge and the waterfall, and I will take care of the rest. Oh, and if anyone believes your name to be the Marquess of Carabas, then play along.'

Well, the lad was confused. But, the next morning, bright and early, he did as he was told. He was splashing in the river's chilly water, when the king's golden carriage trundled by.

'Help!' came a cry. It was the cat, leaping from the bushes. 'Help! The Marquess of Carabas is drowning!'

'Oh, I say!' exclaimed the king. 'Not dear old Carabas!'

He ordered his servants into the water to save the drowning

man – who was, of course, the miller's son. When the lad was safe, the king asked Puss how the marquess had come to be in such a pickle.

'Your majesty,' said the cat, 'while my master was taking his morning swim, he was set upon by a band of cut-throats—'

'Intolerable!' snorted the king.

'And these devilish brutes, with daggers and eyepatches, roughed him up—'

'Insufferable!' spluttered the king.

'And stole his clothes from under his very nose!'

'Inexcusable!' barked the king. He sent a servant to fetch the marquess the finest clothes from the royal wardrobe.

Then, once dried and dressed, the marquess was invited to ride in the golden carriage with the king and the princess. Now, the lad was already a handsome young man. But dressed in the king's silks he was a sight to melt a princess's heart. Which is precisely what happened. The princess took one look at him and tumbled head over heels in love, and he took one look at her and was bowled over by her beauty.

Puss, meanwhile, ran on ahead. He met a group of workers cutting corn in a field.

'Say this field belongs to the Marquess of Carabas,' he warned them, 'or he'll mash you into paste and spread you on his toast.'

Then Puss met a gang of lumberjacks chopping trees in the woods.

'Say these woods belong to the Marquess of Carabas,' he

warned them, 'or he'll dice you into mincemeat and stuff you in his sausages.'

Finally, Puss met a group of washerwomen scrubbing clothes in a stream.

'Say this stream belongs to the Marquess of Carabas,' he warned them, 'or he'll chop you into teeny-tiny pieces and feed you to the fishes.'

And just behind the cat was the king in his carriage. He asked the workers, the lumberjacks, and the washerwomen who owned the land. Frightened by Puss's threats, they replied: Carabas, Carabas, Carabas.

'Gosh!' thought the king. 'This chap is even richer than I am!'

As evening fell, Puss reached a magnificent castle, which belonged to a fearsome ogre. This ogre was rumoured to have a very rare skill: the ability to take any shape he wanted.

'The rumours aren't true, are they?' the cat asked him. 'You can't really turn into any animal you choose, can you?'

Puss said it in such a doubtful tone, that the ogre was irritated.

'Of course it's true!' he said grumpily. And to show he wasn't fibbing he turned into a lion. Puss jumped onto the mantelpiece.

'OK, OK, I admit it: that was pretty impressive,' said the cat. 'You've shown you can change into a big animal. But, of course, you are big yourself. I don't suppose you could turn into a little creature. A mouse, for example.'

'Oh, you don't suppose, do you?' snapped the ogre.

'Well, frankly,' said the cat, calmly cleaning his claws, 'I have my doubts.'

'Right, that's it!' the ogre roared. 'Watch this!'

And he turned himself into a tiny mouse, no bigger than a holly leaf. Instantly, Puss pounced, springing off the mantelpiece and catching the mouse by the tail. Then quickly he swallowed the mouse in one gulp before the ogre could change back.

Presently the king arrived at the castle and Puss hastened to greet him.

'I say, what a splendid place,' said the king. 'To whom does it belong?'

'Why, it belongs to my noble lord, the Marquess of Carabas,' replied the cat.

The king was flabbergasted. He had never known one man to be so stupendously rich. Turning to the lad, he said, 'Carabas, old chap. You have a humdinger of a castle. You have fields and woodlands and streams. You are as pretty as a peacock in your silks and shiny shoes. You would make the perfect husband for my daughter. Say the word and it shall be so.'

The young man did say the word, for he was madly in love, and the happy couple were married the very next day.

And Puss, the cleverest of cats, never had to hunt or lie or scheme again. Although, of course, he did – just for the fun of it.

Cat and Mouse in Partnership

· German ·

The cat in this story, borrowed from the Brothers Grimm, does not intend to be naughty. He has a genuine liking for the mouse. Unfortunately, he has an even stronger liking for food, leading him, with typical feline fickleness, into trickery and dishonesty. One misdeed breeds further misdeeds until there is no turning back – culminating in an inevitable tragic end.

Nevertheless, for all its crimes, the cat in this tale is weak rather than monstrous. The same cannot be said for other cat creatures in German folklore, however. The Tatzelwurm, a giant lizard-like beast from the Alps, has the face of a cat and lethally poisonous breath. Hinzelmann, a malicious kobold – or household spirit – often takes the form of a cat. And then there is the Poplitzer Popelmännchen: a statue of a cat on Poplitz Castle that changes, each midnight, into a small grey goblin with fiery eyes.

Once upon a time, a friendship blossomed between a cat and a mouse. They didn't care one jot about the bad blood between their species; they liked each other, and that was all that mattered. They set up home in a cosy basement and were very happy together. The mouse, a jovial fellow, kept their spirits up, telling stories and cracking jokes, while the cat, who had a practical head on his shoulders, kept the larder stocked and their home

The Mischievous Cat

shipshape and Bristol fashion. In this way, the months passed happily. Their days were spent gathering food and supplies, and in the evenings after dinner they would sit by the fire, playing chess and reading tales long into the night.

All would have been delightful, were it not for one problem: the cat, a worrywart, knew that winter was coming.

'We must prepare for the hard times,' he told the mouse, 'and have a store of food. We will touch it only in our hour of need.'

The mouse thought this an excellent plan, so they bought a pot of fat and hid it in a cubbyhole in a nearby church, where it would never be found. And they swore that neither of them would touch a drop of it until all the other food had gone.

However, one morning, holed up in their den, the cat had a sudden hankering for fat. It started out as a little whisper at the back of his mind, and he tried to ignore it, for he had made a promise to his friend. But the hankering grew stronger and stronger, until he could bear it no longer. He *had* to have a taste.

'My cousin has had a kitten,' he told the mouse, 'and I am to be its godfather. I must go to the christening.'

Of course, there was no cousin or kitten or christening, and as soon as he reached the church, the cat went to the cubbyhole and fetched the pot of fat. He licked all around the top and down the sides, where the gunk had oozed out. Then he returned to the den.

'How was the christening?' asked the mouse. 'And what is the dear child to be called?'

'The kitten's name is . . . Top-Off,' the cat replied.

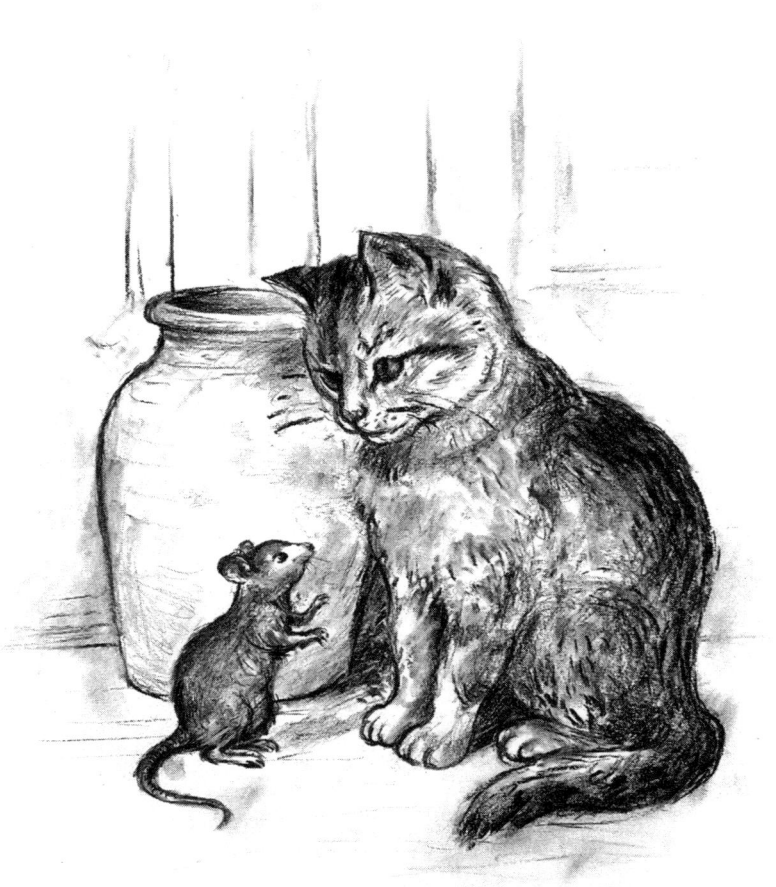

'What a funny name,' laughed the mouse and thought no more about it.

But a week or so later, the cat had another craving for fat, and this time he didn't even try to fight it.

He slunk out of the door, saying, 'Got to go! I have another christening. I'm to be a godparent again.'

Once more, he went straight to the nook and brought out the pot. Unscrewing the lid, he shoved his paw inside and licked the sticky, gooey fat from his fur. He did this again and again, until half the pot was gone.

When the cat returned home, the mouse asked, 'What is the darling child to be called?'

'The kitten's name is . . . Half-Gone,' the cat replied.

The mouse chuckled, saying, 'You cats have such colourful names.'

A few days later, the cat awoke with such a yearning for fat that he was out of the door before the mouse had even risen.

'Bye!' he called. 'Off to a christening!'

And this time, when he held the pot in his paws, he guzzled the fat until none was left – not a single, solitary drop.

That night, when the mouse asked the kitten's name, the cat replied, 'All-Gone.'

And he didn't feel half as guilty as he should have.

Then winter came, as it always does. It grew colder and colder. A bitter wind whipped through the streets and snow fell in heavy drifts, burying the town in white. The cat and the mouse looked high and low, but there wasn't a morsel of food to be found.

'It's a good thing we have that pot of fat,' said the mouse. 'Let's have it now, otherwise we'll starve!'

The cat tried to make excuses – it was too chilly, too icy, too early. But the mouse was famished and refused to wait.

The cat was rather quiet as they headed for the church, and when they pulled the pot from the cubbyhole he feigned surprise to find it empty. But the mouse did not buy it for a second; the cat's guilt was written over his face as plain as day.

'Aha!' squeaked the mouse. '*You* ate the fat! Now I understand: Top-Off, Half-Gone and—'

The words 'All-Gone' were on the tip of its tongue when the cat pounced and, friend or no friend, gobbled the poor mouse down.

The Cat and the Birds

· Classical ·

This story is adapted from one of Aesop's Fables: *a collection of tales attributed to Aesop, an Ancient Greek storyteller. Nowadays, it is generally assumed that the figure of Aesop is an invention, nothing but a convenient name for animal tales to accumulate around. Whether he was a historical figure or not, the fables that survive in his name are an extraordinary collection of tales: charming, funny and wise.*

In this story, the cat displays its usual trickery, and for the usual purpose: food. Here, however, the cat's intrigues do him no good at all. For, as the fable tells us, a villain may disguise himself, but he will not fool the wise.

There was once a cat who lived near an aviary. The aviary was a large cage, in a beautiful leafy garden, and inside dwelled hundreds of delicious-looking birds. This cage drove the poor cat mad. He tried digging under it. He tried breaking open the door. He tried squeezing through the bars. But nothing worked. No matter what he attempted, he couldn't get his claws on the birds. He never caught so much as a single one. Not even a budgerigar.

One day, however, while lurking near the aviary, the cat heard a lovebird sneeze. Then it heard a cockatoo cough. Then it heard the rose-ringed parakeet blow its nose in a hanky.

'Aha! This is my chance,' the cat thought, for he was a wily beast. 'I'll pretend to be a doctor – and cure their sniffles once and for all!'

The cat put on a white coat, found a smart briefcase, and draped a stethoscope around its neck – the whole palaver. Then it knocked on the aviary door.

'Can we – *cough* – can we help you?' croaked a lovebird.

'The question, my friend, is can I help you?' said the cat, drawing his face into a horrible grin. 'I'm a doctor, you see, and I heard that you were feeling under the weather.'

'A doctor, eh?' said the bird, peering suspiciously at the cat.

'That's right.'

'Fully qualified?'

'Most assuredly!'

'Come to cure us?'

'Indubitably. Now, is there anything I can do to help?'

'Yes,' said the bird. 'You can clear off and never come back. If we never see you again, we'll be as right as rain.' Then it slammed the door in the cat's face.

So the cat never did catch so much as a single bird. Not even a budgerigar.

The Clever Cat

· Berber ·

The Berber peoples are the original inhabitants of the Maghreb region of North Africa. Over the centuries, Berbers adopted both the Islamic faith of the incoming Arab populations and the reverence and love for cats common among Islamic societies.

Cats are abundant throughout North Africa; you will see them in medinas and markets, homes and mosques. Many of these cats are strays. This does not mean, however, that they are neglected, for there exists a long-standing tradition of locals leaving leftovers out for them in the evenings.

This story was included in The Orange Fairy Book *– one of twelve volumes of tales known collectively as* Andrew Lang's 'Coloured' Fairy Books. *Lang described the story as a* Conte berbères *– that is, a traditional Berber folk tale – and most likely learned it via the work of French author and orientalist René Basset.*

Once upon a time, not so very long ago, a man died destitute, leaving his son and widow nothing but a falcon, a hound and a cream-coloured cat. The falcon, though pretty, was a petty, jealous bird, and the hound, I'm sorry to say, was rather dim-witted. But the cat was a very clever creature, with a head full of dreams and schemes.

It was most fortunate that the lad had these animals. Without them he and his mother would have starved, for it was only the animals' hunting skills that kept the humans' bellies full of food and a few coins in their purses.

So, one morning, with the larder empty, the lad took the animals into the desert to hunt. The hound dragged down a gazelle. The falcon caught a bird. The cat ran into a barn and poached three rats.

An ogre watched on, admiringly.

'What a lucky young man you are,' it said, approaching the lad. 'I could use luck like that. If you swim to the bottom of the lake, you'll find a trove of silver and jewels. We will divide the spoils between us.'

Though the young man was frightened of the ogre, he agreed to do as the creature asked – for a treasure trove would come in very handy.

He dived into the lake. At the bottom he found four great mounds of silver, jewels and precious gems, shimmering in the water. On top of the largest mound he saw a strange stone, smooth and white, on which were carved all manner of odd markings.

To the lad's shock, the stone spoke. 'I can make all your wishes come true,' it said.

'*All* my wishes?' wondered the lad, gobsmacked.

'All,' confirmed the stone, hearing the boy's thoughts. 'But whatever you do, never part from me for so much as a second. And don't let that ogre see me.'

The lad plucked up the stone, hid it in his pocket, and swam back to the shore.

'Where's the treasure?' roared the ogre, when he saw the lad return empty handed.

'Oh, it was pretty dark down there,' said the lad. 'I couldn't find anything.'

'You saw no treasure?' asked the ogre. 'No nothing?'

'No,' lied the young man, not wishing to reveal he had found the stone. 'No treasure.'

'Not even a white stone, perhaps?' asked the ogre, suspiciously.

'A stone?' said the boy, pretending to think. 'I don't think so. Sorry.'

The ogre stormed off, seething with rage. No sooner had he gone than the lad closed his eyed and made his first wish.

'I wish for a mighty camel and clothes fit for a king,' he said.

'So be it,' said the stone.

When the lad opened his eyes, he was astride an enormous camel and draped in gorgeous golden robes. He galloped home, eager to show his mother. But she was not impressed.

'What's all this?' she scolded. 'You can't afford such finery! Go on, tell me the truth – you stole it?'

'No, no, nothing like that, Mum,' said the boy.

'Nonsense! I always knew you'd come to no good. You're a good-for-nothing – just like your father!' said his mother. 'You pinched it, didn't you?'

'No, Mum,' insisted the boy. 'The riches are mine, fair and square.'

'A son of mine! A bandit!' lamented the woman. 'The shame! The shame!'

'Mum, can you stop that, please!' cried the boy. 'Now, go tell the king I wish to marry his daughter. And promise him anything he asks for.'

'I'll do nothing of the sort!' snorted the woman. 'You, marry a princess?! Imagine!'

'*Please*, Mum,' insisted the boy. 'Just deliver the message.'

His mother thought he'd lost his senses – not that he'd had many in the first place, she muttered – but eventually she did as he asked.

At the palace she requested an audience with the king.

'Your majesty,' she said. 'My son desires your daughter's hand in marriage. In return, you may have anything you ask for.'

The courtiers laughed. How could the son of a peasant woman marry a princess? But the king, a gracious man, did not wish to embarrass the woman, so he said, 'Your son may marry my daughter if he can build me a palace of ice. It should be warmed by the glow of a hundred fires and ring with the song of birds.'

The next day, when the king awoke, his window looked out on a towering palace of ice, its turrets gleaming in the morning sun. A hundred fires burned in its hearths and the song of a thousand birds drifted over the desert.

'Begad! The lad must be a great wizard!' thought the king. 'With powers like that, he could make me a fortune. He'd be a fine son-in-law, peasant or not!'

So, to the courtiers' consternation, the king agreed to the marriage. The young man was wed to the princess the very next morning. They made their home in the palace of ice. With

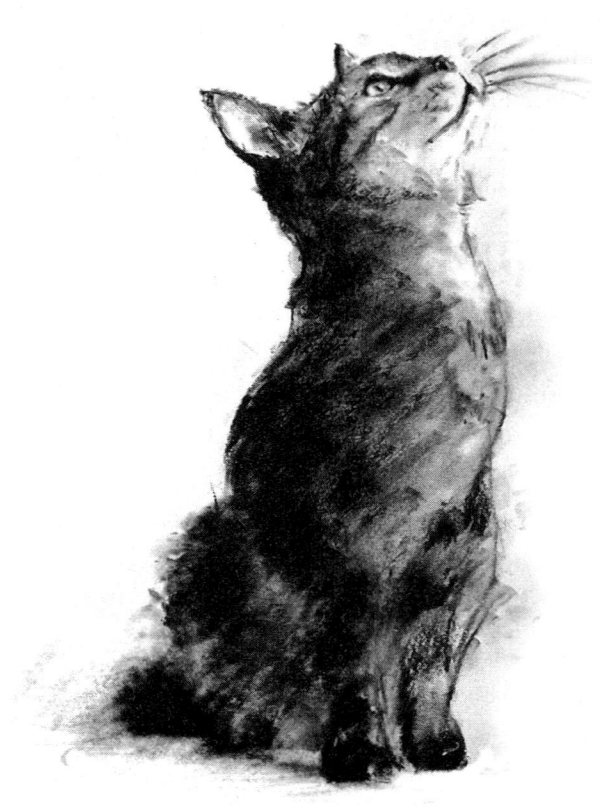

The Clever Cat

the help of the white stone, the lad showered his wife with clothes and jewels and presents. For a time, they were blissfully contented.

But the lad was not used to being cooped up in a palace. He soon grew restless.

'Cat, I need to *do* something,' he said to his very clever cat. 'Come on, find the falcon and the dog – let's go hunting.'

They set off into the desert.

Unfortunately, however, the ogre had learned of the lad's marriage, and his spectacular palace, and now knew the boy had lied about finding the stone. He was determined to have it. So, the very moment the boy and his animals were out of sight, the ogre arrived at the palace gates. Disguised as a jewel merchant, he showed the princess a wondrous collection of diamonds and pearls. Desiring them all, she asked how much they cost.

'Oh, you can't buy them with money, your highness,' explained the ogre. 'But your husband has a white stone. Fetch me that stone and you'll have all the jewels you could ever want.'

When the lad returned from his hunting trip, the princess said, 'Husband, darling, tomorrow is my birthday. I'd like a very special present.'

'Of course, my dear,' said the lad, clasping her hands in his. 'Name it and you shall have it.'

'You promise?'

'I promise.'

'Well, I once saw a very pretty white stone of yours,' she replied. 'I'd like *that* for my birthday present.'

The Mischievous Cat

The lad's heart sank. He knew he must never part from the stone for so much as a second. But a promise is a promise. Sick to his stomach, he handed the stone to his wife, begging her to keep it safe.

The next morning, when the lad went hunting, the ogre returned. The princess swapped the white stone for a barrelful of jewels. But no sooner had the ogre left than all manner of rum happenings beset the palace. The ceiling dripped, the walls ran, and the fires petered out. The songbirds fell silent, then fluttered from the window, never to return.

By the time the young man returned from his hunt, the ice palace had melted away. He found his wife slumped in a pool of water in the middle of the desert.

He understood at once. 'The stone!' he cried to his wife. 'You gave away the stone!'

She nodded, too ashamed to speak.

Without another word, the lad turned and strode into the desert. He was followed by his falcon, his dog and his very clever cat.

'I *must* get the stone back,' he said to his animals. 'Cat, you and the falcon will find the ogre and reclaim my stone.'

The cat hopped onto the bird's back, and together they flew into the air. They soared over the desert and over the mountains, until they found the ogre's castle.

Next to it, the cat spied a den of rats.

'Land here,' the cat told the falcon, 'and I'll have a word with those rodents.'

Their landing caused such panic, however, that it was impossible to talk to the creatures.

'Calm down, you fools! If I wanted to kill you, you'd be dead already!' the cat hissed. 'I just want to ask a favour.'

The leader of the rats poked its head from a hole. 'A favour? From us?' it said. 'Anything! Just don't eat us.'

'Fine. I want you to take three rats and burrow under the castle walls,' the cat explained. 'Then, once the ogre is asleep, you must steal a white stone from his person.'

The rats, scared stiff of the cat, did just this. The next morning, the cat woke to find the stone balanced on its belly.

Pleased with the night's work, the cat and the falcon began the journey back to their master. But the cat was heavy, and the falcon soon needed to rest. It landed on a riverbank.

'Perhaps I should hold the stone for a bit,' suggested the falcon, feeling envious.

'Why? I found it,' said the cat. 'I should carry it.'

'Give me a turn!'

'No chance!'

'Go on!'

'No!'

The bird squawked and the cat hissed and in the squabble the stone slid from the cat's paw and plopped into the lake. It fell straight into the ear of a massive fish.

'Quick! After it!' cried the cat, diving into the water. But it was no match for the fish, who soon disappeared up the river.

'We'll never get the stone back now,' grumbled the falcon, as the cat pulled itself, dripping and sodden, from the water.

But the cat did not give up so easily. It began to scrabble at the ground. Soon it had created a great pile of dirt, which it pushed into the river.

'Oi!' shouted a silver fish, who happened to be passing. 'You're clogging up our water!'

'What do I care?' shrugged the cat. 'I don't live there. I'm going to fill it until there's no river left.'

'But that's madness!' cried the fish. 'We'll all die!'

The cat, raising an eyebrow, said, 'Well, I suppose I *could* stop. But only if you fetch the white stone from the fish who stole it.'

The silver fish agreed. It shot off upstream, asking all it met if they had the stone. Eventually it asked a big green fish.

'Hmm,' said the big fish. 'Something *did* fall into my ear a while back. It might be a stone, or it might not. Hard to say.'

The silver fish peered inside the big fish's ear and plucked out the stone. Then it swam back to the cat and spat the treasure onto the bank.

Delighted, the cat and the falcon returned to the young man. The lad danced ecstatically when his stone was once more safely in his possession.

'Oh, you clever, clever cat!' he laughed, sweeping it up in his arms and kissing its furry head. 'You really are the most remarkable of beasts!'

And then the young man wished for another palace. But, this time, it wasn't built of ice. No, this time it was built from sparkling green marble, and, to the best of my knowledge, it stands there still, home to the lad, his princess, and the very clever cat.

The Cat and the Mice

· Tibetan ·

In life, as in literature, mice are cats' most frequent victims. This, unfortunately, is a fact to which most cat owners can attest – many have woken to find a loving 'gift' on the floor.

In this tale from Tibet, the ageing cat must employ its ruses and wiles to catch the creatures, proving, once again, how untrustworthy cats can be. It was included in Folk Tales from Tibet *(1906) by W. F. O'Connor, an Irish diplomat and officer, who spent several years travelling the country eliciting stories from, among others, 'village headmen, monks, servants, local government officials, peasants and traders'. He claimed to transcribe and translate these oral tales just as he heard them, with no knowledge of their age or origins.*

Interestingly, a similar tale was told by the Persian poet Ubayd Zakani in the fourteenth century. There, a cat is overcome by guilt after killing a mouse. He turns to religion and, after much praying and fasting, vows to never consume another mouse. When the mice hear of this promise, they visit the cat to offer their gratitude. The cat, however, is peckish after his long fast – and devours all the mice. The parallels between the two tales (and, indeed, with the Palestinian story 'The Cat as Holy Man') reveal the widespread recognition of the cat's fundamental deviousness.

The Cat and the Mice

There was once a very old spotted tabby who lived in a farmhouse. In her youth, the farmhouse had been close to heavenly, for there were mice here, there and everywhere. There were so many mice, in fact, that she had grown fat and lazy – just as every cat wishes to. But now her joints were stiff, and her eyes were weak, and each day it grew harder to catch enough mice to fill her belly.

One morning, she was struck by a cunning idea. She invited all the mice in the farmhouse for a meeting. They were nervous at first, of course, but after she promised not to eat them, they slowly gathered around.

'Now, my little friends,' she began, 'I've got an announcement to make. I've been doing a lot of thinking lately, for I am growing old and have begun to look back on my life. I've realised that I've behaved awfully – simply *awfully* – to you poor, dear little creatures.'

The mice looked at each other in confusion.

'No, really,' the cat went on, 'I've been a very wicked cat. And to make up for all the harm I've done, I'm going to spend my remaining years in penance and religious contemplation and . . . whatnot. Praying and meditating. That sort of thing. Consequently, I hereby swear never to eat another mouse in my life!'

The mice let out a cheer of delight.

'But there's one *tiddly* thing I ask for in return. Each morning and each evening, you must all come and thank me for my generosity, one by one.'

The mice agreed to this at once, of course. After all, it sounded far better than being eaten.

And, so, twice each day, morning and evening, the mice formed a procession and filed past the old moggy, thanking her as they passed. And, twice each day, morning and evening, the old cat waited for the procession to pass . . . and then snaffled the last mouse in the line.

'Ha!' thought the cat. 'My body may have slowed, but my mind's as quick as ever! These foolish creatures are literally lining up to be eaten!'

It went on like this for some time: the mice filing past, the cat eating the last in the line, and the mice never even noticing.

As the weeks went by, however, two mice became suspicious. These mice, Rambé and Ambé, were brothers, and were somewhat smarter than their fellows.

'Brother, how come the cat doesn't eat but never grows thinner?' wondered Rambé.

'Good question, brother. And doesn't it seem a bit quieter around here recently?' said Ambé, looking around. 'Didn't there used to be more mice?'

They agreed that the entire business felt shady. After much discussion, the pair hatched a plan: one of them would walk at the front of the procession and the other at the back, and, as they marched, they would call to each other. That way, if anything happened, they could shout out a warning.

So, the next morning, when the time came to pay thanks to

the cat, Rambé took his place at the head of the line, and Ambé took his place at the rear.

'Ambé?' called Rambé as he walked.

'Here!' replied his brother. 'Rambé?'

'Here!'

And they kept this up the whole way. The cat, perplexed, decided that eating the last mouse as usual would be too risky. What if the mouse cried out and ruined her crafty scheme?

'Bother!' she muttered, feeling hungry. 'But never mind, it's just one meal. I'll catch a mouse in this afternoon's procession.'

But, that afternoon, Rambé and Ambé did exactly the same.

'Ambé?' called Rambé as he walked.

'Here!' replied his brother. 'Rambé?'

'Here!'

And, just as before, the cat went hungry.

'Bother!' she spat, ravenous now. 'This can't go on! If I don't eat tomorrow, I'll waste away!'

That evening, the two brothers warned the other mice about the cat.

'You can't trust her!' insisted Rambé.

'Be ready in case she pounces,' advised Ambé.

So, the next morning, the mice were all on their guard. Rambé and Ambé performed their plan as before.

'Ambé?' called Rambé as he walked.

'Here!' replied his brother. 'Rambé?'

'Here!'

The cat was livid. 'Not this again! I can't bear it any longer! I need some food!'

With a snarl, she pounced. She sprang on the procession of mice. But, thanks to the brothers' warning, they were prepared. Before the cat could nab one in her jaws, the mice had all scurried off to safety.

From that moment on, the mice never trusted a word the cat said, and the cat never caught another mouse for the rest of her days. The cat, growing older and hungrier, died soon after – but whether from old age or starvation, it's difficult to say.

The Fox and the Cat

· Classical/German ·

The story of an animal with many tricks who is outdone by an animal with only one trick is an ancient one. It has enjoyed many iterations, featuring in, among others, the writings of Greek poet Archilochus in the seventh century BCE, an ancient Indian collection of animal fables known as the Panchatantra, *and the eighth-century Persian work* Kalīla wa-Dimna. *However, in the West it is best known for its inclusion in both* Aesop's Fables *and* Grimms' Fairy Tales. *In these versions, we see a horribly smug fox being bested by the more prudent cat.*

Through these many retellings, the animals featured have varied, with hedgehogs often playing the role of the 'sensible' creature. The moral, too, has been interpreted in numerous ways: that it's better to have common sense than cleverness; that knowledge is worthless if you don't act on it; and, perhaps, that you should always beware fools with pretensions of greatness.

A cat took a walk down a dingley dell. It was minding its own business, looking for food, when it chanced upon a fox. The fox was an arrogant, calculating creature, and the cat knew better than to upset it.

'Good morning, dear fox,' the cat said amiably. 'I hope this lovely day finds you well?'

The Mischievous Cat

The fox threw its head snootily in the air and stared down its nose at the cat. It had such a disagreeable gleam in its eye, that the cat was quite put out.

'You dare to talk to me?' the fox hissed. 'You – you – you bundle of fur. You mouse-eating, whisker-licking, tail-swishing cat. What do you know of art, of culture, of philosophy? What do you know of talent, wisdom and flair?'

The cat mulled this over. 'You may well be right,' it said, unconcerned. 'I don't know much. But I do have one very handy skill.'

'And what is that?' snapped the fox.

'When the hounds chase me, I jump into a tree, where I am as safe as safe can be.'

'You call that a skill?' sneered the fox. 'Why, I have a whole bag of skills. I have more ways of escaping the hounds than there are twigs in a forest. In fact, only the other day I—'

The fox, busy boasting, failed to notice that the hunter and his hounds were upon them. The cat bounded into the tree with one great leap. But the fox was caught in the dogs' jaws and could not break free.

The cat, lazing on the branch, watched idly as the fox struggled.

'Why don't you use something from your bag of skills?' it purred, swishing its tail. 'Why don't you use your talent, wisdom and flair?'

But the fox was dead and never replied, while the cat sunned itself in the tree, as safe as safe can be.

4
The Companion Cat

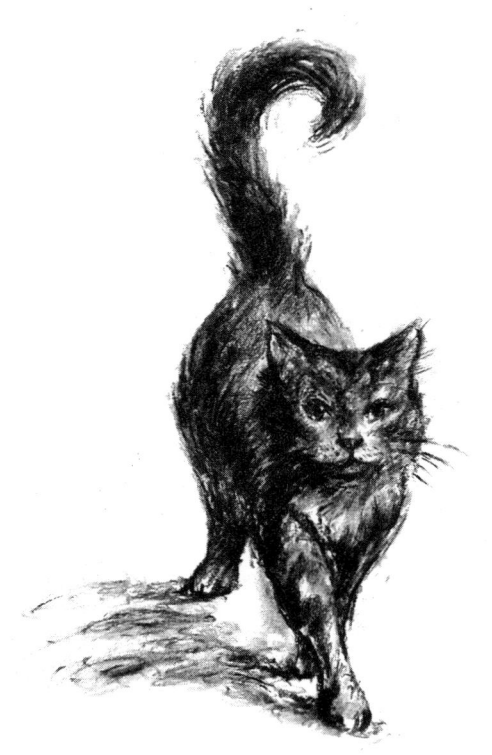

Some would argue that our relationship with cats never evolved into true companionship: that even thousands of years after they started catching the rodents that plagued our grain stores, it remains a marriage of convenience; that cats simply tolerate our presence in their homes, suffer our strokes and attentions, in return for warmth, safety and food.

But that rings false to anyone with a cat. A cat's love is subtle and reserved – unlike the more demonstrative dog, with their needy barks and jumps. Cats do not try to impress you. They do not try to please you. They do not do anything because they are meant to, or you want them to, or you have told them to. No, cats show their love in exactly the same manner they do anything: how and when they please. If a cat offers you affection it is because, at that moment, they want to offer you affection. It's pointless to demand attention from a cat. They are just too proud, too independent. All we can do is be patient.

Because when the love does come, it is more than worth the wait. There are few things in life better than a warm cat curled up on your lap, its purr rumbling away, its soft fur between your fingers. That is why we suffer the scratched doors, the litter trays, the panicked visits to the vets. It is why we forgive the early-morning wake-ups, the midnight zoomies, the dead mice on the kitchen tiles.

So even if, as some say, cats love us only because they need us, that does not matter. After all, we love them only because we need them: for companionship, comfort, warmth.

There are many different types of companion cats. Happy

cats and grumpy cats. Lazy cats and crazy cats. Shy cats and show-off cats. Cats who never seem to wake up, and cats who rarely come home. Cats who love everybody and cats who love nobody. Some cats are mercurial; there is no predicting where they'll turn up. Others are creatures of habit, choosing the same laps every evening, the same beds each night. Some cats sense when you are feeling low and need a cuddle. Some know when you are returning home and wait to greet you. Some cats (if you are very fortunate) doze on your lap as you write books.

The companionship that cats offer may be on their terms. But that does not diminish it; if anything, it makes it more meaningful. They choose to share their love with us. And in doing so, cats improve our lives immeasurably. The love of a cat can save people from loneliness; help them battle mental-health issues; and make the world a brighter, warmer, more welcoming place.

The cats in this chapter demonstrate a selection of the different sides of the companion cat, and the different roles they have played in human lives, from the Animal as Helper motif so common in fairy tales – such as in 'Dick Whittington and His Cat' – to 'The Cat's Elopement', in which a princess's life is saved by the cat's talent for hunting. Unlike the magical cats of so many fairy tales, however, the animals in these stories are flesh and blood. They help not by being supernatural but by simply being cats.

Not that any assortment of stories could sum up the extraordinary and complex relationship between us and our cats.

The Cat's Tales

And so, 10,000 years after they first pounced on a rat in a grain store, that is why we still agree with the ancient Egyptians: the cat (though maddening, and ridiculous, and exasperating) is truly the perfect companion.

Dick Whittington and His Cat

· English ·

One of the most well known of English folk tales, 'Dick Whittington and His Cat' is based on a historical figure. Richard Whittington (1354–1423) was born into a wealthy family. As a young man, he became an apprentice in the City of London, where he learned the trade of mercer. He must have learned well, for he became so rich that soon he was lending money to King Richard II himself and later to King Henry IV.

Whittington used his resources to gain a series of offices, eventually rising to be Mayor of London. On his death, Whittington bequeathed his entire fortune to charity.

This generosity secured his place in folklore. Though only loosely based on fact, his story has been told and retold countless times over the centuries. Since its first appearance as a play in 1604, it has been a ballad, a chapbook, an opera and innumerable works of prose. It is now firmly established as a pantomime favourite.

Just how and why a cat snuck into the story is unclear. But it does not matter a great deal. After all, what story isn't improved by the presence of a cat?

Dick Whittington's parents died when he was very young. He was taken in by his neighbours: kind-hearted people who did all they could to help him. But it was a poor village in a poor time, and there were many mouths to feed. Rarely could they spare more than a few crusts of bread or some leftover soup.

It was a grim, unhappy life, and one day Dick decided to seek his fortune in London – a magical place, he had heard, where people, rich as lords, walked streets paved with gold.

'I'll just pick my fortune off the floor,' he thought, 'and I'll never go hungry again!'

Dick packed his few possessions into a knapsack and headed to London. For ten days and nights he walked: across patchwork fields, down cobbled lanes, through villages of thatched cottages, until, footsore and weary, he reached the city.

But London was nothing like Dick had dreamed. The city was dirty and loud and smelly. Instead of streets paved with gold, they were caked with filth and horse dung. Instead of elegant lords and ladies gracefully walking the streets, there were heaving crowds, shouting and rushing, bustling and fighting. On every corner and in every alley there seemed to be a beggar or a half-starved child, pleading for a coin or two.

Cold and hungry, Dick huddled in a doorway, seeking shelter from the wretched night. As he slipped into a dismal sleep, the owner of the house returned. The man, a wealthy merchant, asked Dick his business.

'I'm sorry, sir,' sniffed Dick. 'But I'm a poor orphan; I have no home and no family.'

Happily, the merchant had a generous spirit. He welcomed the lad into his house, offering him supper and a bed for the night. The next morning, Dick was found a job in the kitchens, chopping carrots and washing dishes.

Dick had never been happier. The kitchen was warm, his belly full, and the merchant and his daughter, Alice, were the best of people. All was not perfect, however. He soon discovered that the cook was an awful bully; she walloped him with her ladle every chance she got. And the attic in which Dick slept proved infested with rats. At night, the clatter of their claws on the floorboards stopped Dick from sleeping.

One morning, Dick, bleary-eyed from lack of rest, saw a girl selling kittens on the street.

'Aha!' thought Dick. 'That's just what I need. The cat will get rid of the rats for me.'

But Dick had no money – not even so much as a penny in his pocket. So, he began to shine shoes before work each morning. By the end of the week, he had earned enough to buy a kitten: a beautiful grey cat with white splotches on its fur.

Dick and the little cat became the best of friends. The boy shared his meals with the cat, giving it half of everything. And he shared his bed, for the cat curled up on his chest, warmer than any hot-water bottle. And he shared his hopes and dreams, telling the cat how one day he would make his fortune and marry Alice, with whom he had fallen in love.

And in return, the cat hunted rats. She was a marvellous mouser and poached and pounced until not even a single rodent remained in the attic.

Now, the merchant was a kind and honest man, but he had one rather strange rule. When he dispatched a ship to faraway lands to buy and sell goods, he made each of his servants place one of their possessions on the ship. His crew would then sell those possessions on the voyage. That way, the servants shared his risk, but also his reward, for sometimes they too grew rich.

When the merchant told Dick of this rule, the boy was worried. 'But I have no possessions, sir,' he told the merchant. 'The only thing I own in the whole world is my dear little cat!'

'In that case, my boy,' the merchant replied, 'you must hand over your cat.'

Dick begged and pleaded, for he loved his pet, and did not want to part with her. But his master insisted, and so the cat was sent away to sea.

With the cat gone, the rats returned. And the cook, growing meaner with age, walloped Dick harder each day with her ladle.

One night, Dick lay in bed, feeling sorry for himself. His heart was broken from missing his cat, and the clacking of the rats' claws was keeping him awake.

'I wish my cat was here,' he thought bitterly. 'And the rats are driving me potty! There's nothing to look forward to – nothing except a conk on the head from the mean old cook!'

Dick decided that it was time to leave the merchant's house. So, the next morning, he got up before the sun had risen and set off, a knapsack over his shoulder. Dick traipsed through the city until, exhausted, he decided to rest at the top of a hill. He sat down on a stone. As he rested, the chimes of Bow Church

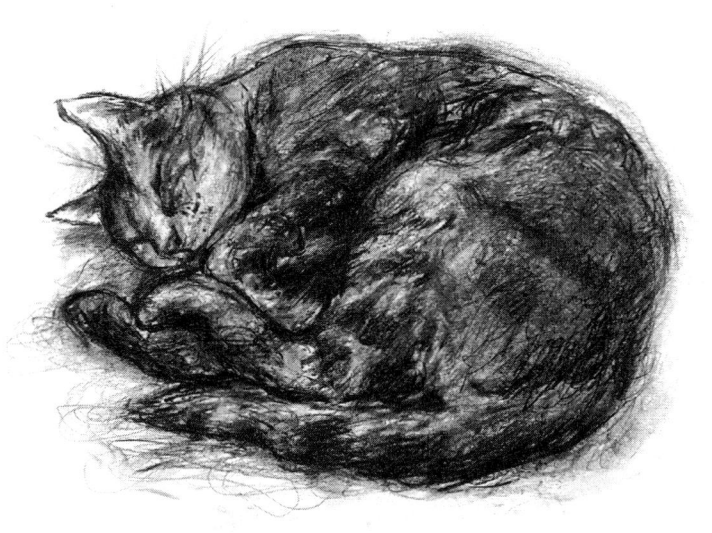

rang out across London. They drifted across the rooftops and the parks, the streets and the trees. To Dick, however, they did not sound like clanging bells. To him, they seemed like voices raised in song:

> Turn again, Dick Whittington,
> Three times Mayor of London Town.

'Me! Mayor of London?' thought Dick, amazed. 'Imagine!' All of a sudden, he was brimming with hope. 'I can stomach all the rats in the world – and even the cook's ladle – if I am to be Mayor of London one day.' And he jumped up and headed back to the merchant's house with a spring in his step.

Meanwhile, Dick's cat had voyaged across the great wide sea. The ship sailed as far as Africa, where it landed on the Barbary Coast. The King of Barbary was keen to buy the ship's cargo and greeted the sailors with a fabulous feast. But as they were finishing their fourth pudding, the hall was invaded by hundreds upon hundreds of rats. The vermin dashed over dishes and jumped into jugs; they scampered across tables and scrambled up tapestries.

'Help! Help!' demanded the king, as he hopped onto his chair. 'Who will rid me of these troublesome beasts?'

The captain of the ship, who was a clever fellow, said, 'Your majesty, we have on board our ship a creature called a cat. She will free you from these pests.'

The cat was brought to the palace. Dashing and darting, bounding and biting, she made short work of the rodents. The king was delighted. He insisted on buying the cat, handing over a ginormous sack of gold in payment. The ship returned to London, laden with jewels and precious metals. And much of that wealth belonged to Dick.

'I offer my congratulations! You are a rich man now, Mr Whittington,' the merchant explained, shaking Dick's hand. 'Nearly as rich as I am!'

Dick's days of being hit on the head with ladles were over. He was wealthy beyond his wildest dreams. He went into business with the merchant and became even wealthier; he married Alice, the merchant's daughter, and they were blessed with many children; and, finally, just as the bells of Bow Church had predicted, he became thrice Mayor of London. And he did a good job, too, building hospitals and schools for the poor, because he never forgot the days when he had known cold and hunger.

Everywhere he went people said, 'There goes Dick Whittington, the finest of fellows!'

To which, smiling, he would reply, 'Oh, I did nothing! Nothing at all! I owe it all to the dearest of creatures – my truly wonderful cat!'

The Cottager and His Cat

· Icelandic ·

This Icelandic tale is a cousin of 'Dick Whittington and His Cat'. Similar tales have been found throughout history and all around the world. They may date back as far as the tenth century and have been found in as diverse places as Italy, Germany, Finland, Persia, Indonesia and parts of Africa.

Why are cats so often depicted making a character's fortune? It seems to be the combination of two ideas, one magical and one mundane: firstly, a variant of the Animal as Helper theme seen so often in fairy tales, and, secondly, an exaggerated reflection of the very real, very practical role played by cats in human society – for, thanks to their poaching skills, possessing a cat really could make a difference to one's livelihood.

This traditional Icelandic fairy tale was first collected in 1864 by Jón Árnason, a folklorist often considered Iceland's answer to the Brothers Grimm.

A miser lived in a ramshackle hovel. He hoarded many bags of gold under his bed and could have lived the life of a king if he wished. But it pained him to part with a single penny, and so his clothes were tattered rags and his shoes were more hole than leather.

When the old man died, his son inherited his fortune. The

young man was delighted, for he had spent his life cold and hungry, and now he could afford to live in comfort.

In his dreams that night, however, a stranger came to him and said, 'Your father's wealth was stolen from the needy. Give half to the unfortunate and toss the other half in the sea. But as the money sinks, be sure to grab anything that swims.'

When the young man awoke, he was troubled by his dream. Had his father stolen the money? Did it truly belong to the needy? The mere possibility was so hateful he felt unable to keep the money; his conscience would not allow it. So that very day, he handed half of the gold to the orphanage in the village. The rest he hurled into the ocean.

As the riches disappeared into the water, the young man spotted a scrap of paper bobbing on the waves. He fished it out. Unwrapping the package, he found six shillings. It was the only money he had in all the world. 'It's not much,' he thought, 'but it's something.'

The young man traipsed through the forest, feeling very sorry for his lot, for he hadn't had a bite to eat all day. As darkness fell, he reached a hut where an old woman lived. She welcomed him, inviting the lad to share her dinner, humble though it was.

The young man took a seat at the table. While he dined on bread and cheese, he noticed a small animal sitting by the fire. The creature had silvery-grey fur, like shadows and moonlight, and pointed ears sent pink by the firelight. Behind it, a long sinuous tail flicked this way and that, seeming to move of its own free will, while round green eyes stared back at the lad, inquisitive and gentle. It was, he thought, the most elegant, most beautiful beast he had ever seen.

'What is that extraordinary creature?' he asked excitedly.

'Why, it's a cat,' the old woman replied.

'It's magnificent!' cried the lad, getting up to stroke the animal. 'How I'd long for one to call my own!'

'Really?' said the old woman, dubiously. 'Well, it's yours for six shillings, if you wish.'

'Ah, if only I could!' the lad said sadly. The cat rolled onto its back and let out a loud purr as the young man smoothed the pale, downy fur on its belly. 'But six shillings is all the money I have in the world!'

Nevertheless, he stared into the creature's moon-like eyes; he stroked its soft, velvety fur; and, before long, his kind heart melted. He *had* to have this creature. So, when he left the next morning, he was one cat heavier and six shillings lighter than the night before.

But now, of course, he had no money at all. He wandered from village to village, from hamlet to hamlet, passing through valleys and woods, fields and meadows. He was often hungry and always footsore and tired. But everywhere he went, his little grey cat helped him to make friends, for everyone loved to pet the cat's soft fur, and play with the lively, affectionate creature.

At last, the youth came to a castle where a great king lived. He asked for an audience, hoping to offer his service and find work. But, when he entered the hall, he was astounded to see it overrun with black vermin, with mean teeth and thin, furless tails.

'The pesky things are called rats,' the king explained, seeing the young man's bewilderment. 'And they are a confounded nuisance. I would give my kingdom to be rid of them!'

At that, the young man's cat, snug in his coat, burst out and scooted across the table. There was a great commotion: a whirlwind of fur and claws and teeth. In a moment or two, a great heap of rats lay dead. The remaining rats scarpered, whizzing up drainpipes and whooshing down holes. Soon the hall was free of the pests.

The king was jubilant. 'What a phenomenal beast!' he declared, ruffling the cat's head.

Turning to the young man, he said, 'For the service you have rendered me, I will give you a great reward. You can either be my prime minister and run the country, or you can marry my daughter and become king. Which shall it be?'

The young man looked at the prime minister, who was grey and haggard. Then he looked at the princess, who was young and fair.

'I will marry your daughter and become king,' he said.

And he never regretted his choice.

The Cat's Elopement

· Japanese ·

Japan is a cat-loving country. Cats are simply everywhere. They are in cat temples and cat museums. They are on cat islands and at cat festivals. They're in comics and books, TV shows and films. They're on clothes and keychains, toys and trinkets.

They are even in shop windows. Take a stroll down a Japanese street, and you will find cats waving to you from shops and restaurants, for the maneki-neko, *or 'beckoning cat', is a fixture of many businesses and households. These small figurines, depicting a cat with a raised paw beckoning to passers-by, are talismans believed to bring fortune to their owners.*

Indeed, cats are generally considered a symbol of good luck in Japan. Certainly, by saving the princess's life, the cats in this tale prove themselves the bringers of good fortune. They also enjoy good fortune themselves: for this is the story of a star-crossed love triumphing over adversity – a rare example of cats, usually solitary creatures in traditional tales, being afforded a relationship with their own species.

'The Cat's Elopement' has its roots in oral Japanese folklore, but was introduced to Britain by Andrew Lang in 1897, itself an adaptation of a German version by David Brauns.

Two cats, named Gon and Koma, were madly in love. Gon was a handsome, white-furred tom; Koma, a slender, tortoiseshell queen. Their owners would not let them marry, however, for Gon came from a wealthy home and Koma from a poor one, and neither wanted to mix with the other. The human households tried to stop the two cats from meeting. During the day each would spray their neighbours' cat with water if they found it in their garden and at night they would lock their doors to keep their pet inside.

But the cats' love would not be thwarted. They always found an opportunity to sneak out of their houses. Every night they would meet in the moonlight at their special place: the branches of a bright red maple tree.

'My love, whatever shall we do?' declared Gon one night. 'I cannot bear another day without you!'

'And I cannot bear another minute without you!' wailed Koma.

'Well, then you won't have to!' decided Gon. 'Let us run away and get married!'

'Oh, yes, let's!' cried Koma, nuzzling her lover with her cheek. 'But when?'

'Why, now, of course!' said Gon. 'This very moment!'

So that night, the two cats eloped, slipping off into the moonlit woods. Happy and carefree, they walked until sunrise then stopped to rest beneath a cherry tree. It was a beautiful morning. The sun shone; birds sang in the trees; a stream burbled nearby. The two cats felt happy and free.

A growl disturbed their bliss. Standing before them was an ogre. It had taken the shape of a ginormous black dog, with fangs like knives and great strings of drool swinging from its jaws.

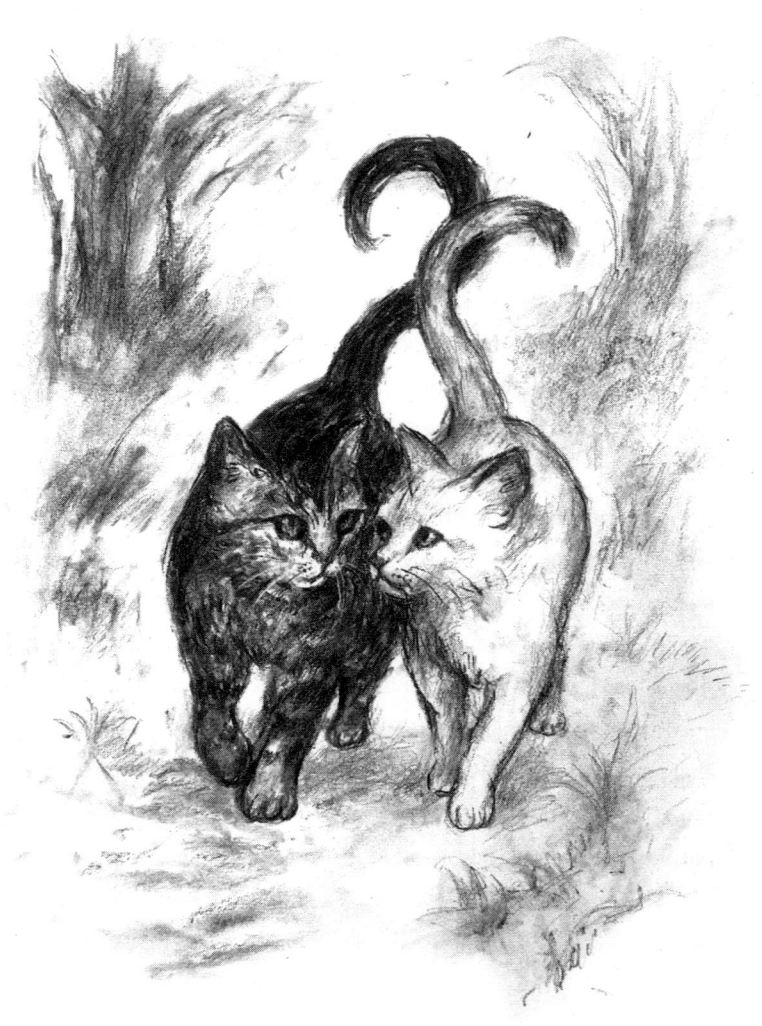

The Cat's Elopement

Koma sprang deftly into the cherry tree. But Gon stayed rooted to the spot. Whether he was too thunderstruck to move, or too brave to run, I couldn't say. The dog was ten times his size, however, and would have made short work of him if Koma hadn't shouted for help.

A gardener heard Koma's cries. Swinging a shovel around his head, the man chased away the snarling ogre. Then, before Gon could join Koma in the tree, the gardener, immediately taken with the fine-looking cat and not noticing the other, swept him up in his arms. He took the cat to live in a princess's palace, thinking it would make a fine gift for her. The princess was kind, but Gon longed for Koma and dreamed of the day they would be reunited.

One morning, the princess was playing her koto. Dreamily, she plucked a slow, peaceful tune on the zither-like instrument. Entranced by the music, she failed to notice a venomous snake worming its way towards her. The serpent slithered up her leg, up her arm, and onto her shoulder. In fact, it wasn't until the very moment the snake was about to sink its fangs into her neck, that the princess felt its scales on her skin. She shrieked, waking Gon, who had been dozing nearby. He leapt across the room and, with one snap of his jaws, severed the snake's head from its body.

The princess now loved Gon more than ever. Pampered and petted, he was the luckiest cat in the world. Or, at least he would have been, if it weren't for the pain of missing Koma so dreadfully.

A few days later, Gon was napping in the garden when he was woken by a yowl. A thuggish tom was bothering a little cat.

Gon detested bullies. He charged through the flowerbeds and scared away the rascal.

And then, to his astonishment, he realised that the little cat was Koma. The adoring couple greeted each other rapturously.

'My love!' Gon cried, rushing to Koma's side, utterly delighted.

'My darling!' she sobbed, rubbing his cheek with hers. 'I feared I'd never see you again!'

The couple made such a fuss – purring and mewing and touching noses – that the princess grew curious. She hurried over to meet the new cat.

Gon and Koma told the princess the story of their love. The princess, moved by their tale, promised they would never be parted again. And they never were. The couple had a kindle of kittens; and the princess married a prince and had children; and the two families were happy until the end of their days.

Venus and the Cat

· Classical ·

In this story, included in Aesop's Fables, Venus, the Roman goddess of love, is persuaded to transform a cat into a human, so the cat can win the love of her owner. All runs smoothly until the cat-woman inadvertently reveals her feline self – the moral being that it is impossible to hide one's true nature.

The tale has another interesting feature: the cat is hopelessly devoted to her owner. Despite their reputation for aloofness, this bonding to one particular person is actually a common characteristic of cats. They often bestow their affections on one, and only one, member of the household, with the rest being treated with a detachment that borders on indifference. This favouritism is revealed in various ways, including exposing their bellies, licking hair, head bumping, and rubbing. Most of all, of course, it is demonstrated by who they choose to be near – whose lap they sit on, or where they sleep.

A beautiful black cat lived with a young man. He was a handsome youth, with piercing eyes and wavy hair. But this young man wasn't only handsome, he was considerate and kind. He always offered the cat titbits from his own plate and spoke loving words when he scratched her belly. Soon, the cat had fallen hopelessly in love.

The Companion Cat

Every morning, the cat hopped onto the man's bed and watched him sleep. 'I wish he loved me as I love him,' she thought.

Every afternoon, the cat rubbed against the man's legs as he scribbled away at his desk. 'I wish he loved me as I love him,' she thought.

Every evening, the cat sat on the man's lap as he read by the glow of the fire. 'I wish, I wish, I wish he loved me as I love him,' she thought, as the man smoothed her fur.

Venus, the goddess of love, heard her wish.

'So, you love this man?' the goddess asked the cat.

'I do,' the cat nodded.

'You want him to love you back?'

'More than anything in the world,' the cat purred.

And so – just like that! – Venus turned the cat into a human. The beautiful cat with black fur became a beautiful woman with black hair. One glimpse of her, and the man was smitten.

A year passed, and Venus, in an idle moment, remembered the cat-who-was-now-a-woman. Out of curiosity, she decided to pay her a visit. Venus watched as the young couple ate dinner. Then she watched them curl up on the sofa, the man stroking the woman's hair.

'She certainly looks like a person,' thought the goddess. 'But does she behave like a person?'

And she conjured up a mouse and set it loose in the room.

The cat-who-was-now-a-woman lost her head. She forgot that she was a human. She forgot her loving boyfriend. She forgot all manners and decorum and civilised behaviour.

Instead, she darted across the room, pounced, and caught the mouse in her teeth.

'Ah, nature will out,' tutted Venus. Disgusted, the goddess promptly changed the woman back into a cat.

But cat or woman, she never stopped loving the handsome young man.

Silvershod

· Russian ·

Cats are good luck in Russia. According to superstition, hearing a cat sneeze on your wedding day is a promise of a happy marriage; a cat rubbing a paw on its face ensures a visit from a welcome guest; and the first creature to enter a new house should always be a cat, for their presence will bestow good fortune on the owners and the home.

And, in a way, this is exactly what the cat in this story does: brings prosperity to its owner. The story originated in the folklore of Siberia's Ural Mountains, where miners and prospectors told of a mythical creature named Silver Deer or Silver Hoof – in some versions a deer, in others a goat. The oral legend was then worked into a fairy tale by Russian writer Pavel Bazhov in the 1930s.

An old hunter lived in the woods. A kind man, he had lived a good life and in many respects he was content: he loved the peace of the forests; and he loved his home, a comfy dacha far from civilisation. But as the years passed, he began to regret that he had no one to share his life with: no one to kiss goodbye when he went out hunting each morning; no one to help pull the snowy boots off his aching feet when he returned each night. So, with the dark winter evenings feeling lonelier by the day, he decided to adopt an orphan. Then, he thought, he would have someone to love – and someone to love him in return.

Silvershod

The old hunter visited an orphanage. He was particularly taken with one girl: a young, rather scruffy slip of a thing named Dara. At first, the girl was so shy she couldn't say a word. She simply sat, cradling her cat on her lap. A tiny calico – white and black and ginger – Moura was her dearest friend in all the world.

When the old man asked Dara if she and Moura would like to come and live with him, the girl didn't know what to say. Her parents had died when she was very little, and she could not remember a life before the orphanage. The long dormitory with its rows of beds, the cold school room, the dining hall where they ate in silence – these were all she knew. But as the old man talked, gently and good-humouredly, he told her such captivating stories about the forest in the wintertime, and his cosy cabin, and the exciting adventures they would share, that she began to like him very much. Best of all, he told her of a magical stag, Silvershod. This white stag, he said, had a silver hoof with a magical gift: it could summon jewels to appear in the snow.

So, Dara agreed to live in the hunter's cabin. There, she and Moura were very happy. Dara loved the old man, for he was gentle and kind; and Moura – an adventurous cat – enjoyed exploring the forest, chasing birds and squirrels to her heart's content. And, of course, the old man was delighted, for now he had someone to kiss goodbye when he went out hunting each morning, and someone to help pull the snowy boots off his aching feet when he returned each night.

One morning, cooking pancakes, Dara saw a white blur shoot past the window.

'Silvershod!' she shouted, bubbling with excitement. But when she rushed to the doorway, there was no stag, just the falling snow and the whisper of the wind in the trees.

That night, tucked up in her bed with Moura on her belly, she heard a loud clattering from above.

'What's that?' she thought, rubbing her eyes. 'It sounds like a creature on the roof!'

She dashed outside, not even bothering to pull on her boots.

A white stag jumped from the roof and stood facing Dara. It was breathtaking. Its coat was as white as new-fallen snow and its solid silver hoof winked in the moonlight. Dara opened her mouth to speak but no sound came out. She could only hug herself in wonder.

Whether they stood like that for a minute or an hour, Dara never knew. The world was silent; snow fell slowly; the girl's heart thudded in her chest. But, eventually, Silvershod huffed the air from its nose, shook the feathery snow from its head, and bounded into the darkness.

The little girl, delighted, danced barefoot in the snow.

The next morning, however, Moura was missing. Dara searched the cabin, and she searched the garden, and she searched by the stream, but there was no trace of her little calico cat.

'Don't worry, my dear,' said the old man, squeezing her shoulder. 'She'll turn up.'

Dara went to look in the forest. 'Moura?' she hollered, tapping the cat's food bowl with a spoon. 'Moura? Please come home, my darling!'

Silvershod

She looked all day, growing ever more frantic, for she loved the little cat more than she loved anyone except the dear old man. Finally, she reached a clearing atop a small hill. There, in the middle of the clearing, stood Moura. Facing her – to the girl's great surprise – was Silvershod. Heads close, the cat and the stag appeared deep in conversation.

Suddenly, the stag pawed at the ground with his silver hoof. An astonishing number of gems tumbled onto the snow, twinkling and glinting.

At that moment the old man, returning from a hunt, entered the clearing. He stood dumbfounded, observing the scene. But he must have stepped on a twig, or perhaps his ragged breathing was too loud, for some sound disturbed the animals. Moura let out a long, maudlin cry and, without warning, the two beasts disappeared.

Neither was ever seen again.

Shaking his head in wonder, the hunter piled the jewels into his hat.

'Can you believe this, my dear?' he laughed. 'Who would ever have thought? Me and you – as rich as the tsars themselves!'

There were diamonds and rubies, emeralds and garnets, and precious stones so rare he didn't even know their names. The old man was about to scoop up the final few jewels, when Dara stayed his hand.

'Can we leave them here?' she asked. 'Just overnight. They look so pretty sparkling in the snow – like little stars! – it's such a shame to move them. Please?'

'Well, I suppose it will do no harm,' chuckled the old man, amused by the child's strange fancy. 'They'll keep here, well enough. We can get them tomorrow.'

But the next morning, when they returned to the spot, the jewels were gone. No amount of searching could bring them back.

It did not matter much, however. Dara and the old man had more than enough for their needs. They could live happily for the rest of their days – and happily they did indeed live, for now they each had someone to love, and someone to love them in return.

But whether the jewels made up for the loss of her beloved cat, only Dara could say.

5

The Greedy Cat

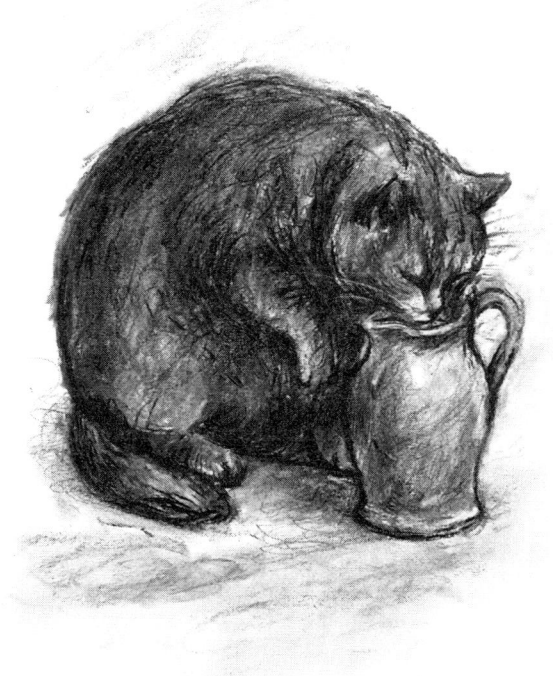

In truth, the majority of the cats in this book, and in folklore generally, could be placed in this chapter. While the cat is a versatile animal in fairy tales, it seems their greed is universally acknowledged. Whatever other qualities the characters possess, most display a love of food – getting their paws on more is frequently their prime motivation and the catalyst for the stories themselves.

When the cats are cunning, it is to gain food. When they are malevolent, it is to gain food. When they are unfortunate, it is because they have *failed* to gain food. Even the helpful cats, such as Dick Whittington's, are driven by their stomachs. While such hunger is occasionally portrayed as natural and healthy, more often than not it is excessive, even dangerous. In many of the tales, it is greed that pushes the cats to dishonesty, or leads them to humiliation, defeat or death.

Greed and hunger are recurring themes in fairy tales. In part, this is a product of the distressing conditions that existed during the era in which many of these stories emerged. In 'Hansel and Gretel', for example, the children's abandonment is the consequence of a famine, and the story is an examination of the extraordinary lengths to which hunger can drive people. To modern readers, such events may seem unrealistically extreme, but in an era of hunger, of poverty, of child abandonment, the problem of too many mouths and not enough food was genuine and pressing. And there are numerous other fairy tales where overwhelming hunger leads to atrocious, previously unimaginable, acts: Rapunzel's mother, for instance, experiences cravings so powerful that she and her husband give up their child, as does the mother in this collection's 'The White Cat'.

In other stories, it is not the hunger that is dangerous, but the food itself. Indeed, from Eve's forbidden fruit to Persephone's pomegranate seeds, from Sleeping Beauty's poisoned apple to the perilous fare of Fairyland, food can be hazardous, even fatal in literature. This has been attributed, in part, to ancient taboos surrounding what one should and should not eat. But it is also because, in stories, food has long represented all manner of other forces: desire, temptation, avarice. A partial list of food-related motifs in fairy tales would include: being cursed for not sharing food; getting trapped in supernatural realms for eating food; food proving magical; food transforming; a never-ending supply of food; characters being threatened with becoming food themselves.

Given the prevalence of food and greed in fairy tales, then, it is inevitable that the topics would feature in stories containing cats – for cats are monstrously, almost ludicrously, gluttonous. This, of course, is a fact all cat owners know. Cats seem to possess bottomless pits rather than stomachs, pits that can never be filled, no matter how much you pour into them. To live with a cat is to become familiar with the early-morning meowing, pestering for breakfast; the pinching of food while you are not looking; the trailing after you, begging for treats; the indiscriminate snaffling of the scraps beneath the table.

And if your cat appears capable of eating almost anything, it is because it can. In the home, they will take whatever is on offer, from chocolate and cheese to porridge and cereal. In the garden, they will occasionally help themselves to plants and grass (which, as an emetic, helps them bring up furballs). At heart, though, cats are carnivores – and hunters. Indeed, without meat, and the amino acid taurine it contains, cats will go blind. Left to their own devices, a cat will target mainly small mammals, especially mice, voles and shrews. But, if the opportunity presents itself, they can also stomach rabbits, reptiles, butterflies, birds and fish, and are even partial to insects, spiders and snakes.

However, the cat's impressive hunting skills pose a major problem to wildlife. This, of course, is no fault of the cats; they are simply doing what cats do. It does, however, go some way to explaining their reputation for remarkable greed. Their gluttony takes many forms in this chapter: in 'The Black Cat', the cat's hunger is opportunistic; in 'Catafay and the Fox', the hunger is ferocious and savage; in 'The Cat and the Cock', the hunger is deceitful; and in 'The Greedy Cat', it is simply voracious – for the cat will, literally, eat anything and everything.

The Greedy Cat

· Scandinavian ·

This Scandinavian story is an example of a cumulative, or chain, tale. In this type of story, common among fairy tales, the action and dialogue repeat over and over, each time accumulating. That is, with every new element introduced, all the previous examples are repeated. Songlike, fun and often silly, cumulative tales are found in cultures all around the world.

Here, the story catalogues the increasingly impossible items a voracious cat has eaten.

A version of this story was first collected in the nineteenth century by Peter Christen Asbjørnsen, one of the great exponents of Norwegian folklore. Together with his collaborator, Jørgen Moe, Asbjørnsen travelled the length and breadth of Norway, seeking and recording traditional oral tales. These were then retold and published in a series of works, beginning in 1842 with Norwegian Folk Tales.

There was once a very greedy cat. It had eaten a bowl of porridge and a blob of jam for breakfast. But it was still hungry, so it jumped out of the window and went looking for more.

The cat saw a farmer mowing a field.

'Good morning,' said the farmer. 'Have you eaten today?'

'Just a smidgeon,' said the cat. 'A bowl of porridge and a blob of jam. I'm still rather peckish though – so I think I'll eat you too.'

And it munched and crunched the farmer.

Then the cat met an old woman knitting.

'Good morning,' said the old woman. 'Have you eaten today?'

'Just a morsel,' said the cat. 'A bowl of porridge, a blob of jam, and a farmer mowing a field. I'm as hungry as a horse though – so I think I'll eat you too.'

And it champed and chomped the old woman.

Then the cat met a postman delivering a letter.

'Good morning,' said the postman. 'Have you eaten today?'

'Just a sliver,' said the cat. 'A bowl of porridge, a blob of jam, a farmer mowing a field, and an old woman knitting. I'm positively famished though – so I think I'll eat you too.'

And it chewed and chawed the postman.

Then it saw a sleepy cow chomping grass.

'Good morning,' mooed the sleepy cow. 'Have you eaten today?'

'Just a crumb,' said the cat. 'A bowl of porridge, a blob of jam, a farmer mowing a field, an old woman knitting, and a postman delivering a letter. I'm still half starved though – so I think I'll eat you too.'

And it mashed and mushed the sleepy cow.

Then the cat heard a barbershop quartet singing.

'Good morning,' sang the barbershop quartet. 'Have you eaten today?'

'Just a mite,' said the cat. 'A bowl of porridge, a blob of jam, a farmer mowing a field, an old woman knitting, a postman delivering a letter, and a sleepy cow chomping grass. I'm absolutely ravenous though – so I think I'll eat you too.'

And it bit and bolted the barbershop quartet.

Then the cat spied a fox with a fiddle.

'Good morning,' said the fox. 'Have you eaten today?'

'Just a pinch,' said the cat. 'A bowl of porridge, a blob of jam, a farmer mowing a field, an old woman knitting, a postman delivering a letter, a sleepy cow chomping grass, and a barbershop quartet singing. I'm so starving I could faint though – so I think I'll eat you too.'

And it nipped and nibbled the fox with a fiddle.

Then the cat saw an oak tree stretching out its branches.

'Good morning,' murmured the oak tree. 'Have you eaten today?'

'Just a speck,' said the cat. 'A bowl of porridge, a blob of jam, a farmer mowing a field, an old woman knitting, a postman delivering a letter, a sleepy cow chomping grass, a barbershop quartet singing, and a fox with a fiddle. I'm as empty as an octopus though – so I think I'll eat you too.'

And it scoffed and scarfed the oak tree stretching out its branches.

Then the cat saw a fluffy cloud floating on the breeze.

'Good morning,' whispered the cloud. 'Have you eaten today?'

'Just a lick,' said the cat. 'A bowl of porridge, a blob of jam, a farmer mowing a field, an old woman knitting, a postman delivering a letter, a sleepy cow chomping grass, a barbershop quartet singing, a fox with a fiddle, and an oak tree stretching out its

The Greedy Cat

branches. I'm rapacious and voracious though – so I think I'll eat you too.'

And it gnashed and gnawed the fluffy cloud.

Then it saw the blazing sun in the sky.

'Good morning,' said the sun. 'Have you eaten today?'

'Just a taste,' said the cat. 'A bowl of porridge, a blob of jam, a farmer mowing a field, an old woman knitting, a postman delivering a letter, a sleepy cow chomping grass, a barbershop quartet singing, a fox with a fiddle, an oak tree stretching out its branches, and a fluffy cloud floating on the breeze. I'm all rumbly in my tumbly though – so I think I'll eat you too.'

And the greedy cat gobbled and gorged the blazing sun, and washed it down with the moon, the planets and the stars above.

It was still hungry though.

Catafay and the Fox

· Russian ·

Also known as 'Liza the Fox and Catafay the Cat', this charming Russian tale shows a cat teaming up with one of the other great folkloric animal figures, the fox. This fox in question is Liza or Kumi Liza, a recurring character in Eastern European folklore, featuring as a trickster in the tales of Russia, Bulgaria and Ukraine. Here she meets her husband, Catafay: a wonderfully complacent creature who, like most cats, assumes it is his right to be fed, pampered and waited on.

Catafay is often portrayed as a Siberian Forest Cat: a particularly furry breed, with three layers of coat to help them through the chilly Siberian winters.

As so often with folk tales, it is impossible to accurately date the origins of this story, a Slavic oral tale first written down in the nineteenth century. It is, however, worth noting its close similarities to fellow Russian tale 'The Cat Who Became Head Forester'.

An old man grew tired of his cat, for it was eating him out of house and home.

'If I keep you much longer, I won't be able to feed myself!' grumbled the man. 'I'm sorry, my boy, but you'll have to go!'

And he took the animal deep into the forest and left it there, all alone.

The Greedy Cat

The cat, a spoilt creature, was used to having three square meals a day – plus puddings and treats and snacks. He didn't know the ways of the wild: how to hunt, how to scavenge, how to steal. But he was a handsome chap with a nonchalant swagger. His tail was bushy, his mackerel tabby fur was thick, and around his neck he boasted a shaggy mane, as lustrous and abundant as a lion's. So, when he met a fox in the forest, she was soon smitten.

'It's a pleasure to meet you, sir,' the fox said shyly. 'I'm Liza. May I ask your name?'

'They call me Catafay. I'm the new governor of the forest,' fibbed the cat, with a proud shake of his mane.

Impressed, the fox invited him for dinner in her den. Liza, much to Catafay's delight, provided cream and chicken and fish. And Catafay, to Liza's pleasure, told long and detailed anecdotes about himself. The pair got on famously and, that very night, they decided to marry.

The next morning, as she went to fetch some lunch, the fox met a wolf.

'My darling fox!' the wolf said (for he had a soft spot for her). 'Where have you been?'

'I've been with my new husband, Catafay, the governor.'

'The governor?' said the wolf, wringing his paws. 'Sounds important. May I pay my respects?'

'Are you mad? Catafay is far too fierce, he'd gobble you right up,' said the fox. 'But if you brought him a lamb, he *might* spare your life.'

The wolf bounded off at once to do as he'd been told.

Catafay and the Fox

Then the fox met a bear. And when the bear learned that the fox's new husband was the governor, he, too, asked to meet him.

'Oh, dear me, no – my Catafay is far too fierce, he'd munch and crunch you into tiny pieces,' said the fox. 'But if you brought him an ox, he *might* spare your life.'

The bear, not wasting a second, rushed to fetch the governor his gift. After killing an ox he met the wolf, who was dragging a lamb behind him.

'Where are you heading with that lamb, dear wolf?' he asked.

'I'm taking it to the fox's house. It's a present for Catafay, the governor,' the wolf replied. 'But, dear bear, where are you lugging that heavy old ox?'

'I, too, am honouring the governor,' the bear said. But then, with a shiver, he remembered the words of the fox. He was in no rush to meet a beast who could munch and crunch him into tiny pieces. 'Wolf, my friend, why don't *you* see him first,' he said. 'I will wait my turn.'

'No, no, after you,' said the wolf, afraid to be gobbled right up. 'I insist.'

'No, *I* insist,' said the bear.

They argued for quite some time. Finally, a hare bounced past, and they saw a solution to their quandary.

'Hare, come here!' growled the bear. 'Run and tell the fox that we have our gifts. We will meet the governor by this pine tree.'

The hare hopped off to deliver the message. Meanwhile, the wolf hid in the bushes and the bear climbed the tree. After a while, the bear spied the cat and the fox approaching.

The Greedy Cat

'Ssssh!' he whispered to the wolf. 'The cat is coming.'

'What's he like?'

'In truth, he's rather small – but very fierce. I don't like the look of him one bit.'

When the cat reached the ox, he jumped onto its belly and started tearing and rending with his claws. Then he ate as if his life depended on it.

'Delicious!' he sighed, guzzling and gorging.

'Delightful!' he moaned, chomping and champing.

'Delectable!' he cried, chewing and chowing.

'What a creature!' thought the bear. 'Not even *I* could eat that fast.'

Meanwhile, the wolf, who couldn't see what was happening, heard the grotesque growls and yelps the cat made as he ate. Terrified, he trembled so violently the bush began to shake.

Catafay heard the leaves rustling. 'A mouse!' he cried. And he leapt into the bush, sinking his teeth into the poor wolf's nose.

'Ow!' howled the wolf. 'My 'ose 'urts!'

And he took off through the trees with tears in his eyes.

Meanwhile, the cat (who had expected a mouse and found a wolf) shot lickety-split up the tree in fright and bumped into the bear's bottom.

'Help! Help!' cried the bear, thinking the little creature was attacking him. Crazed with panic, he jumped from the tree. He landed with a thud and fled into the woods.

Well, news spread of the beast who could beat a bear and wound a wolf. All the creatures in the forest, big and small, were

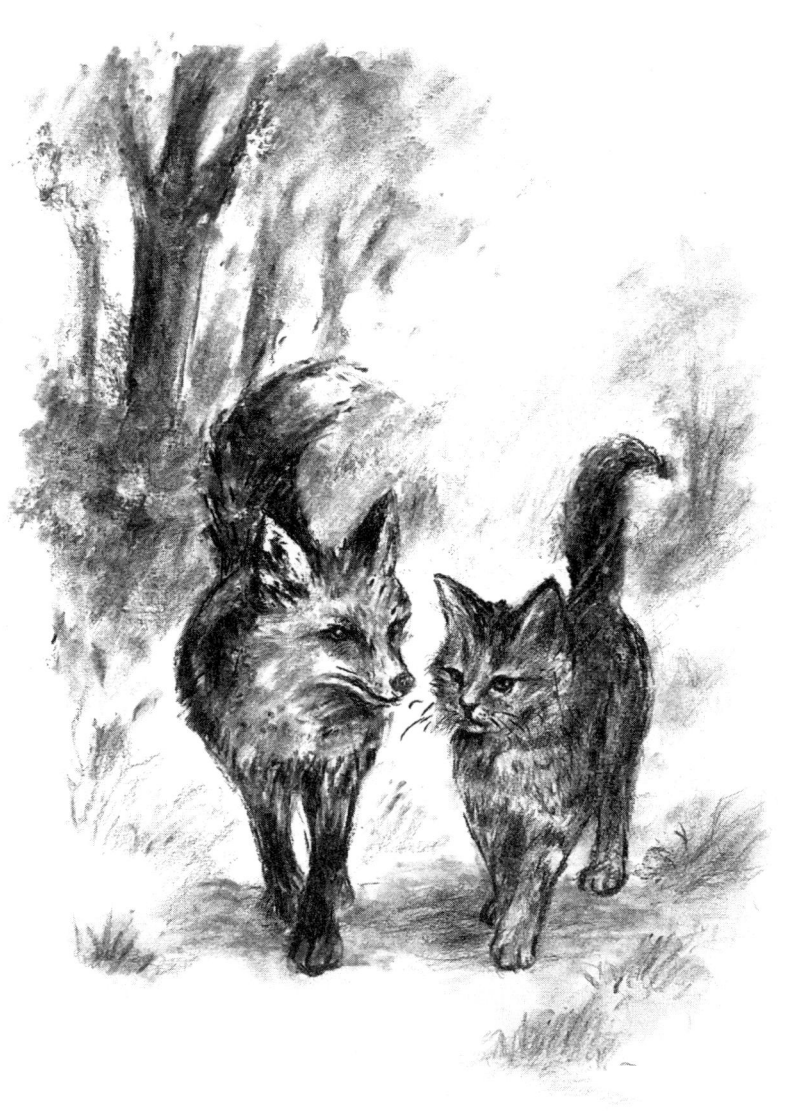

in awe of the cat. Only too keen to keep him happy, they left gifts of food at the mouth of Catafay's den each morning. Now, once more, the spoilt creature had three square meals a day – plus puddings and treats and snacks.

And from that day to this, the greedy cat and the cunning fox never went hungry again.

The Cat and the Cock

· Classical ·

In this story, one of Aesop's Fables, the cat tries and fails to justify his actions rather than admit his greed. The moral of the story: villains have no excuse for their crimes.

The cat was introduced to Ancient Greece and Rome by the Egyptians. At first, the classical world failed to share the Egyptians' reverence for the cat and continued to favour ferrets and weasels for pest control. By the fourth century CE, however, the Romans had enthusiastically adopted the cat. After that, the cat crept into their affections and their myths, as we've seen with both Diana and Venus.

There was once a black-and-white cat who lived on a farm. Though ramshackle and run-down, it was a wonderful place to call home, for there were always rats to chase and barns to explore. She spent her days merrily enough, teasing the chickens and dozing in the hayloft.

Like many farm cats, she was as wild as she was tame. If the farmer remembered to feed her, she would dine on bacon and fresh cream. But many were the days when the old farmer, worn out from a hard day's work, drifted off in his chair and clean forgot.

At such times the cat made the best of things. She caught mice in the barn and rats in the field or ambushed pigeons that

The Greedy Cat

landed in the yard. And, in this way – now being fed, now hunting – she grew comfortable and plump.

However, one winter, the farmer took to his bed with flu and couldn't feed the cat for a week.

'Not a problem,' said the cat. 'I'll find a mouse in the barn.' But she searched the barn inside and out and couldn't find a single mouse.

'Not a problem,' she said. 'I'll catch a rat in the field.' But she searched the field from hedge to hill and couldn't find a single rat.

'Not a problem,' she said. 'I'll snaffle a pigeon in the yard.' But the cat lay in wait all afternoon, and not a single pigeon landed within reach.

By now the unfortunate cat was hollow with hunger. 'What am I to do?' she thought. 'The farmer can't feed me, and I can't catch a thing to eat!'

Just then, a cock hopped into the yard. The bird pecked at the grain on the floor. Now, as a rule, the cat didn't eat the chickens in the yard, for she knew it would make the old farmer angry. But her tummy so ached with hunger, and her mouth so watered at the prospect of a chicken dinner, that she simply couldn't resist. The cat, however, was too proud, or too embarrassed, to admit she was eating the bird out of need.

'I'm not doing this for myself,' she told herself, as she crept up on the cock. 'I'm doing it for all those woken by the cock's crow each morning.'

Sometimes, you see, we tell lies to ourselves as well as to other people.

The Cat and the Cock

Silently, she stalked closer, eyes fixed firmly on the bird. When she was just a few feet behind it, she paused. Crouching low, she wiggled her bum in the air and . . . pounced.

With a great spring, the cat landed on the unsuspecting bird and caught it in her jaws.

'Ow!' clucked the cock. 'What on earth are you doing?'

'I'm putting an end to your racket,' said the cat. 'Every day you wake us with your crowing. Now we can all have a good night's rest!'

The cock was offended. 'If it weren't for my crow, everyone would oversleep!' he said, haughtily, ruffling the feathers on his breast. 'People need me and will be sorry when I'm gone!'

In her heart, the cat knew the cock was right. But she had gone too far to stop now.

'That may be true; or it may not be,' she purred. 'But one thing is definitely true: it's time I had my supper.'

So she gobbled up the poor bird.

And very tasty it was too.

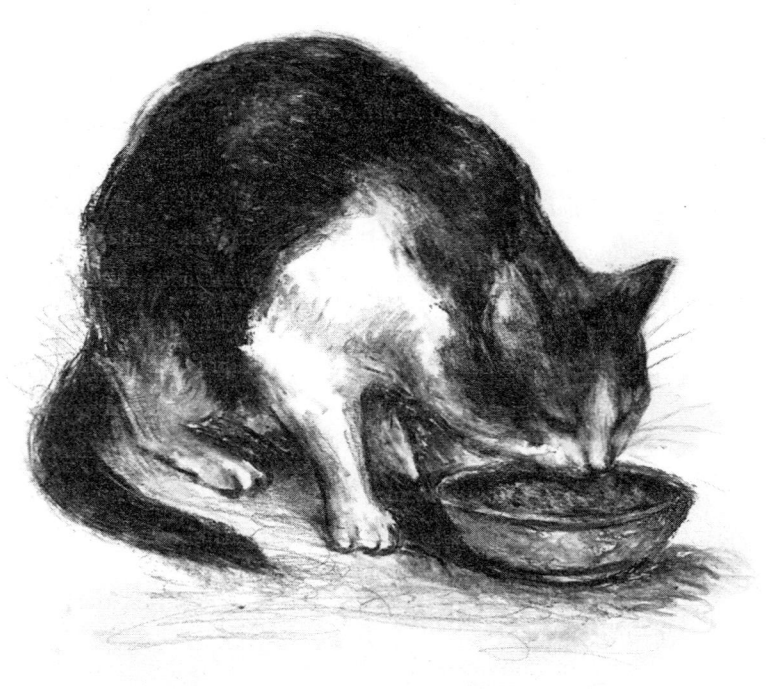

The Black Cat

· Jewish ·

An oral story of Tunisian Jewish origin, this simple tale portrays the opportunism of cats. Turn your back while you are cooking, leave a dish unattended, be so foolish as to lay the table – any of these could, in the presence of a cat, cost you your supper.

Additionally, note the belief that hitting a black cat will cause madness – just one of a number of superstitions surrounding black cats. While in many parts of the world they are believed to be bad omens, in others, confusingly, they are considered good luck: throughout Europe, sailors believed that having a black cat on board would bring the voyage fortune; in England, a black cat given as a wedding gift blesses the marriage; in Japan, seeing one means you will be lucky in love; in Scotland, meanwhile, one appearing in your doorway promises prosperity.

A couple were having dinner one night when a coal-black cat leapt through the window. It hopped onto the table and began to eat, as though it were an invited guest.

The couple were alarmed.

'We must hit the beast and chase it out!' said the woman, reaching for a broom. 'Otherwise, it will eat up all our food!'

'Don't do that, whatever you do!' cried the man. 'If you strike a black cat, you go stark raving mad. Everyone knows that!'

'Nonsense!' shouted the woman. 'Chase it out!'

'Leave it be!' roared the man.

'Chase it out!'

'Leave it be!'

And they went on like that for some time. They bickered, and they battled, but they were both so stubborn that neither of them gave an inch.

And while they quarrelled, the cat wolfed down their dinner and stole back into the night.

6

The Malevolent Cat

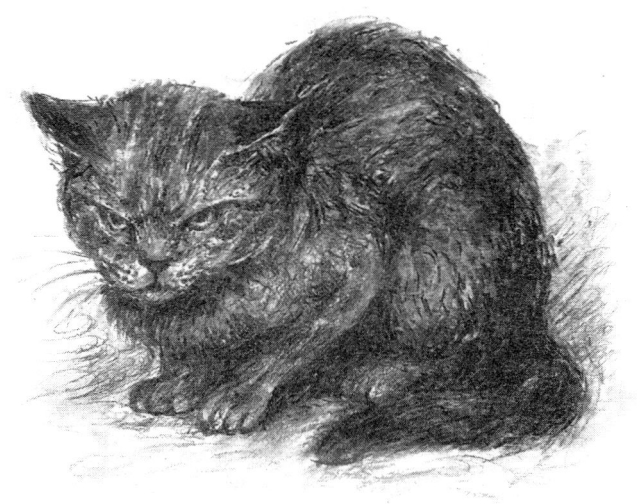

Even cat lovers must acknowledge that cats possess a touch of darkness. We all know cats (although never our own) who carry an air of menace: the cats, perched on a wall, who glare evilly at passers-by; the tyrants who rule, with screeches and scuffles, the neighbourhood's gardens and alleys; the cats who morph from dozing furballs to hissing, clawing demons.

Of all the malevolent cats, the most prevalent is the witch's cat. The relationship between cats and witches has its roots in ancient Greece. Once Hecate, goddess of the underworld, assumed the form of a cat to thwart the giant Typhon's attack on the gods. Disguised, she placed an enchantment upon the monster, allowing Zeus to strike him dead with a thunderbolt. Ever afterwards, the goddess favoured cats, and they became symbols of all she represented, including witches, ghosts and black magic.

Cats also played a role in the worship of Diana, Roman goddess of the night and the moon. Her followers met four times a year for their sabbaths. During these ceremonies, held at night in isolated places, celebrants would impersonate cats, dressing themselves in skins and masks. The cult of Diana survived the collapse of the Roman Empire, and with the growth of Christianity became stigmatised as witchcraft.

Thus, by the Middle Ages, cats and witches were firmly entwined. As with ancient pagan cults, witches were understood to take on the form of cats, both during their rituals, by adopting masks and costumes, but also through actual shapeshifting. Innumerable accounts survive of witches transforming into felines: witches fleeing in the form of cats; witch-cats

The Malevolent Cat

congregating in covens; cats destroying goods and businesses; cats cursing and killing. In Aberdeen in 1596, for example, allegations were made that a group of witches turned into cats and performed unholy rites around a cross in a fish market. Such rumours were rife between the fifteenth century and the middle of the eighteenth, a period that saw a mania for witch-hunting sweep through Europe.

These witch-cats were capable of human speech. They employed this ability to converse with each other, but also to spy on non-magical folk. Consequently, people were loath to allow cats into their home, or even to talk in front of them, in case they were eavesdropping witches.

Many testimonies describe seeing a cat injured, only for the next day a woman to bear identical injuries, thus being exposed as a witch. In the eighteenth century, a man in Caithness, Scotland, reported that a gaggle of cats were talking outside his house. He killed several with an axe, injuring the others. The following morning, the bodies of two women were discovered, while a third woman had an inexplicable gash on her leg. Such events, believed common in real life, naturally featured in fairy tales, with two of the following stories ('The Cat Witches' and 'The Cat-Witch') incorporating this theme.

In addition to being a favourite form for witches to adopt, cats were popular familiar spirits – minor demons who take animal shape and serve as witches' companions. In the Chelmsford witch trials of 1566, Elizabeth Francis claimed to have a familiar named Sathan. In return for a few drops of her blood, this white-spotted cat stole sheep, rendered her husband lame, and killed a man for spurning her love.

However, the employment of cats for nefarious purposes was not limited to witches. Cats have long been believed to feature in satanic rituals. During these ceremonies, often taking place at night in graveyards, devotees would summon demons from hell. The custom commonly included sacrificing a cat, usually black, and draining its blood.

Indeed, black cats are most closely connected with magic and evil. This is a long-standing tradition: Hecate was accompanied by black cats; the Knights Templar were alleged to worship the Devil in the guise of Baphomet, a giant black cat; the Manicheans, a gnostic sect, revered the Devil in the form of a black cat; during the witch-hunts, black cats were feared to have the 'evil eye'; while, in seventeenth-century Russia, the Antichrist was portrayed as having the head of a black cat. Since medieval times, they have symbolised death. It was believed that a black cat on a sickbed, for example, signalled an imminent demise. This prejudice lingers to this day. Many areas of the world, including Russia and China, still regard black cats as unlucky, particularly if one crosses your path.

However, not all malevolent cats can be blamed on witches or the Devil; some cats are simply dangerous in their own right. Cultures all around the world share a fear of giant, monstrous felines – an unsurprising dread given the existence of deadly big cats, in the form of lions, tigers, leopards and jaguars. Some examples of monstrous cats include: Iceland's Jólaköttur, or Yule

The Malevolent Cat

Cat, a gigantic black cat who devours children on Christmas Eve if they have not received new clothing; the *nekomata*, a giant spirit cat from Japan with two tails; the wampus cat, a livestock-killing beast the size of a panther in North American folklore; the bad-tempered splintercat, also American, who flies through the air, crashing into trees; the *cha kla* of Thailand, a black ghost cat, even the sight of whom is fatal; and the South American Hombre Gato, a part-cat, part-human monster who preys on people at night.

This chapter will look at some of the more common malevolent cats: witch-cats, demonic cats, and monstrous cats. They may, quite possibly, remind the reader of some of the bad-tempered cats they know. But never, of course, their own.

King Arthur and the Cat

· Welsh/French ·

The most famous cat in Welsh legend is the Cath Palug (meaning 'scratching' or 'clawing' cat). In Welsh mythology the monstrous cat is said to plague the Isle of Anglesey. With the introduction of King Arthur to the story, however, and the spread of the Arthurian legends into France, the action was transposed further afield, even as far as Switzerland. Likewise, the cat has a number of supposed origins, with tales claiming that it was, variously: the offspring of Henwen, a white pig with the gift of prophecy; a kitten raised by the enchantress Ceridwen; and a punishment from God after a fisherman broke his vow.

In the legends, the cat, a ferocious beast with an impossible appetite, is defeated by a champion. Often this champion is Sir Kay, a Knight of the Round Table, who is dispatched to rid the isle of the creature. He succeeds, but only after it has eaten 180 of his men.

In the following story, however, it is King Arthur himself who battles the Cath Palug. King Arthur, one of the most renowned of all legendary figures, first appears in the written record in the Historia Brittonum *and the* Annales Cambriae, *dating from the ninth and tenth centuries respectively. However, the earliest known account of his battle with the Cath Palug comes from a thirteenth-century French prose romance known as* The Vulgate Merlin.

King Arthur and the Cat

Once there was a great ruler named King Arthur. A mighty king, just and true, he ruled over the Kingdom of Britain. Arthur had performed such wondrous feats of courage and strength that he was loved by his people and feared by his enemies. With his wife, the beautiful Guinevere, King Arthur ruled Britain from the castle of Camelot. There, together with his Knights of the Round Table and the wise wizard Merlin, he watched over his country, protecting the innocent and fighting evil.

This is the tale of one such evil.

One morning, the wizard Merlin arrived with grave news.

'Your majesty,' he said, 'I have heard tell of a great shadow that has befallen the land: a monstrous cat, so terrible and so ferocious, that it is devouring our livestock and our people – whole villages of them.'

'This is serious indeed,' said Arthur. 'Where did the creature come from?'

'It is said that it came from a lake,' said Merlin. 'For once there was a fisherman who promised to give the next fish he caught to God as an offering. But when he pulled his net from the water, he found a fish so large and tempting that he could not bear to part with it. He kept it for himself. "I will give the next fish to God, instead," he promised. But the next fish he caught was even larger and even more tempting. This, too, he kept for himself. "God will have to wait. But this next fish will be for him, I swear," said the fisherman. But the third time he pulled in his net he found not a fish but a small black kitten. "I have more need of a kitten than God does," thought the man, "for, unlike my house, Heaven is not overrun with rats and mice." He took the kitten home, feeding and nurturing it. But the cat, alas, was no ordinary pet. Its appetite was never satisfied, and it never stopped growing, and one night, the beast murdered the man and his family and fled to the mountains. And there it lives now, devouring all that it meets.'

'This monster is most certainly a judgement from God,' declared King Arthur. 'It must be slain without delay. Gather the men.'

That very morning, King Arthur set out, accompanied by Merlin, Sir Gawain and a retinue of soldiers. They rode through valleys, forests, and villages. As they journeyed, they met many who had suffered at the hands of the monstrous cat and could tell stories of its murderous sprees. But as they neared the mountain itself, they found no people at all. They found nothing but deserted homesteads and abandoned hamlets and, everywhere they looked, evidence of great destruction and death. The inhabitants of this region had either fled in fear of the beast – or fallen victim to it.

At last, King Arthur and his men reached the mountain. Grey and craggy, it stretched up to a distant, jagged peak, shrouded in mist. Merlin led them up a steep, rough path, so narrow they could only walk in single file. When they had trekked for an hour or so, the wizard came to a halt.

'Sire, a little further ahead, beneath that outcrop, there lies a cave,' he said to Arthur. 'That dark hole is the foul beast's lair.'

'Excellent,' said the king, readying his spear. 'Now, you must remain here, for I will go alone.'

'But, sire, I must protest!' said Sir Gawain. 'It is too dangerous! Let me accompany you!'

'No, good friend,' said the king, with a firm shake of his head. 'This is a challenge for me and me alone.'

'Very good, your majesty,' said Merlin. 'But ready yourself – for the beast is not to be trifled with.'

While Merlin, Sir Gawain and the soldiers drew back, the king proceeded on foot. He had not gone far, when the cat emerged from the mouth of the cave. Having heard the footsteps approaching, it had come in search of its next meal.

It was more terrible than King Arthur had ever imagined: black as midnight, large as a bison, with dagger-like fangs, long and blood-stained.

With a ferocious growl, the fiend charged at the king. Arthur thrust out his spear, hoping to pierce the beast through the breast. But the monstrous cat caught the spear in its teeth and snapped it as though it were kindling. Then it leapt on the man, knocking him to the floor. Arthur, with a swing of his shield, which caught the cat on the jaw, managed to fend it off for long enough to regain his feet. Springing up, he drew his sword. When the beast next leapt, Arthur struck him fiercely across the breast, drawing blood. The cat let out a great angry shriek, so hideous it hurt Arthur's ears.

Enraged, the demon cat rushed at the king. It sunk its claws straight through the chainmail and into the man's flesh. With a

The Malevolent Cat

roar of pain, the king blocked the next attack with his shield. The cat's claws penetrated so deep into the wood, however, that it could not remove them. They were stuck fast. Seizing his chance, Arthur swung his sword with all his might, severing the cat's front legs at the knees.

But even this did not stop the monster. Rearing up on its hind legs, it sprang on the king, tearing and rending with its fangs. Many blows the king managed to deflect but they were too numerous, and too fast, to defend completely. Soon, his shoulder and his breast were marked with blood, and a great gash jagged across his noble face. Finally, however, the king succeeded in striking a blow of his own: slicing the cat's back paws from its legs.

Now the beast was defenceless. It howled and moaned most piteously. Bloody, crippled, it strove to haul its body back to its cave. But King Arthur, refusing to allow it to escape, buried his sword into the monster's heart.

The cat-monster was dead.

Merlin and Sir Gawain rushed to his aide.

'Your majesty,' cried Gawain, 'are you hurt?'

'Nothing of consequence,' Arthur assured him. 'I will survive.'

'Unlike this foul beast,' said Merlin. 'Surely, this is the Devil himself.'

'Most assuredly,' agreed the king. 'I have fought many a monster – even the great giant of St Michael's Mount – but none ever challenged me like this hellish cat. I feared, in truth, that it would be the end of me.'

King Arthur and the Cat

King Arthur and his companions returned to Camelot. Great were the celebrations when news spread that the monstrous cat was slain. As a reminder of his foe, King Arthur kept the giant paws that had been embedded in his shield, and the mountain was renamed 'The Mountain of the Cat' – a name that endures to this very day.

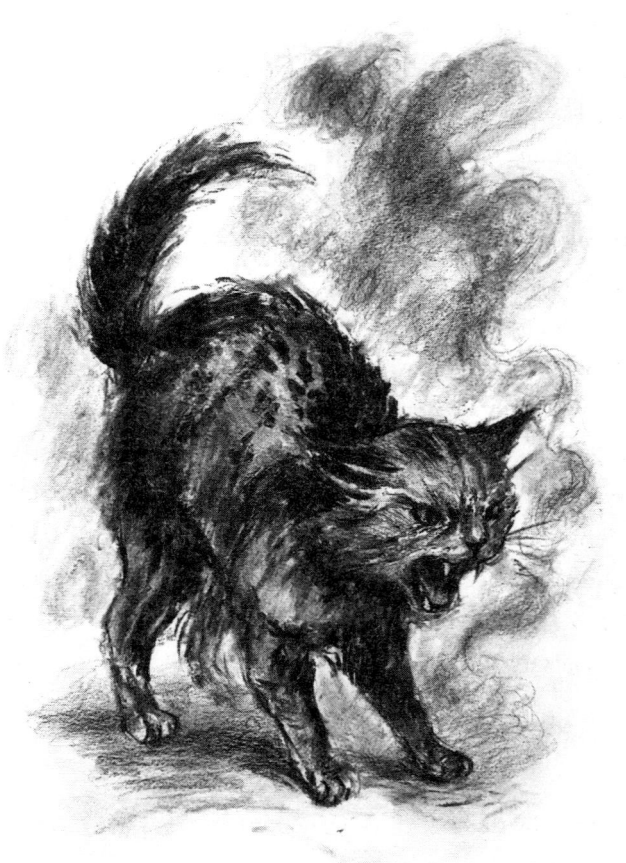

The Demon Cat

· Irish ·

In Ireland, the best-known monstrous cat is the cat sidhe, *or 'fairy cat'. This creature, which also features in Scottish folklore as the* cat-sìth, *is huge and black with a white spot on its chest. Some believe it a demon, others a fairy, and some a witch in disguise.*

The cat sidhe *is known for stealing the souls of the dead. Traditionally, therefore, people went to great lengths to protect bodies while they awaited burial: fires went unlit in the room where the corpse lay, lest the warmth attract the monster, and music and games would be played elsewhere in the house, hoping to lure away the beast.*

The cat sidhe *is a particular danger during Samhain, the Gaelic festival marking the beginning of winter. At this time, the border between the living and the dead dissolves, allowing the fairy cat to prowl between the two. It was customary to leave out saucers of milk, hoping to please the* cat sidhe. *Those who did not would be cursed.*

While not specifically named as a cat sidhe, *the demonic cat in the following tale shares a number of similarities with the monster.*

In a cottage by the sea, there lived a mother and her daughter. One night a great black cat burst through their door, attracted by the smell of mackerel wafting from the kitchen. The cat was so monstrously big the women were aghast.

'It's the Devil! The Devil!' cried the daughter.

The Malevolent Cat

'That's no way to talk to a visitor!' said the cat, affronted. 'Don't you know that name-calling is rude?'

And it gave the girl such a scratch on the arm that she screamed and screamed. A neighbour came running. Bravely, the man set upon the giant feline with a staff. But the cat was a wild ball of claws and teeth. The man was soon sent packing.

Then the cat jumped onto the table and tucked into the family's supper.

'Begone!' barked the mother, picking up a rolling pin and cracking the beast on its back. But the cat simply smiled and continued its meal.

'Really!' tutted the cat. 'You call yourselves civilised creatures.'

Then the mother thwacked it with a broom handle and the daughter smacked it with a poker. Together they rained down blows heavy enough to stun a cow.

'You really do have the most horrendous manners,' chuckled the cat, helping itself to another fish.

Finally, the mother fetched a bottle of holy water from the cupboard. She sprinkled a few drops on the cat's head.

Instantly, a thick cloud of smoke formed, black and acrid, darkening the whole room. The beast wailed in pain, letting out such shrieks and whines that the women's stomachs turned somersaults. There was a sizzling sound, and their nostrils filled with the stench of sulphur.

Two red eyes, like glowing embers, could be seen through the haze. These eyes shrivelled until they were nothing more than pin pricks; then they disappeared entirely.

The Demon Cat

When the smoke had cleared, there was no sign of the cat; no sign, that is, but for a small pile of ash on the floor. Well, the woman swept up the ash and tossed it away and no demon cat ever stole their fish again.

The Cat Witches

· Welsh ·

The following tale concerns Huw Llwyd, a wizard. Though a legendary figure in Welsh folklore, he was in fact based on a historical personage. Born in 1568 near Llan Ffestiniog in North Wales, Huw Llwyd led a storied and adventurous life: fighting as a mercenary in the Netherlands and France; earning a reputation as a bardic poet and harpist; and being renowned as a preacher. But it is as a magician that he is remembered. According to legend, he possessed the ability to heal, to fight demons, and to see into the future. This occult reputation was probably not harmed by his habit of wearing robes adorned with magical symbols and a crown of sheepskin and feathers.

In the centuries after his death in 1630, a number of tales sprang up regarding his exploits: that he punished a crooked innkeeper by placing a spell on his inn, forcing its patrons to dance indefinitely; that he dined on eagle flesh in order to win healing powers for nine generations of his family; and, even, that he never in fact died, but walks among us still.

But best known, perhaps, is this tale, in which the wizard confronts two light-fingered cat burglars.

Everyone knows – or else should know – that the seventh son of the seventh son is a wizard. Huw was such a man. Through his natural gifts and many years of study he grew to be a powerful sorcerer.

One winter's evening, Huw was drinking at an inn when a band of rowdy men approached. Though they pretended to be friendly, the wizard possessed the gift of prophecy and knew that the men planned to slit his throat while he slept and steal his silver. They had, however, picked on the wrong man.

Huw murmured an incantation. Instantaneously, a white tusk sprouted from the middle of the table. Long and spiralled like a unicorn's horn, the magic tusk mesmerised the men. They forgot all about Huw and instead stared in wonder at the marvel. They were still standing there, gawping at the tusk, when Huw left the following morning.

Huw continued to the next village, where he heard talk of a mystery. A nearby inn had suffered a series of thefts. Items had gone missing from locked rooms. No one could fathom how the burglars were getting in and out without being caught.

Intrigued, Huw paid the inn a visit. It belonged to two sisters, who served Huw a lovely stew and plenty of beer, chatting away pleasantly all the while. The wizard was charmed. He was more determined than ever to catch whoever was stealing from the sisters' inn.

When darkness fell, Huw retired to his room and climbed into bed. He did not go to sleep, however. Instead, with a candle burning and his sword hidden beneath the blanket, he waited for the thieves to come.

The Malevolent Cat

The night was cold, and the bed was warm, and it was hard for Huw to fight off sleep. He grew drowsier and drowsier. The waiting seemed to last forever. Many times he heard a noise only to find it was the branches clawing at the window, or the leaves rustling on the trees.

But, as midnight struck, a scratching came from the chimney breast. Someone was coming! Quickly, he lay back and pretended to snore. To his great surprise, he saw two cats creep from the fireplace. They ransacked the room, rummaging in the wardrobe and in his bag.

Then, one of the cats reached inside Huw's coat. The wizard leapt out of bed, seized his sword, and gave the cat a powerful thwack on the right paw. With an ugly scream, the cat scuttled up the chimney and disappeared, its friend following close behind.

At breakfast the next morning, the younger sister was far less charming than the night before, serving the food in a sullen silence. And the older sister, Huw was told, was poorly and confined to bed. Finishing his scrambled eggs, Huw decided to bid farewell to the sick woman. The younger sister tried to dissuade him. She offered all sorts of excuses: that he would catch the flu, that the invalid was not dressed, that Huw would be late on his journey – but the wizard insisted.

He climbed the stairs to her room. It was dark, the curtains drawn. The older sister lay swaddled in blankets. She held out her left hand for Huw to shake but he refused it, wishing to kiss her right hand. When the right was offered, most unwillingly, it was bandaged and bloody. It had, Huw saw immediately, been struck by a sword.

'They're a pair of witches!' thought Huw, startled. 'And they can turn into cats!'

'I made you bleed with a wizard's sword, and that means you can never perform magic again,' Huw told the older sister. 'And now,' he said, turning to the younger woman, 'I will do the same for you!'

And he cut her on the hand – not severely, but enough to cause a line of blood to show.

Then Huw walked out into the rain, knowing that the witches' days of skulduggery had been ended, once and for all.

The Cat-Witch

· North American ·

Cats were brought to North America from the Old World. Unfortunately, so was a fashion for witch trials. One notorious trial occurred in 1692 in Salem, Massachusetts. Of the several hundred people accused, some twenty-five lost their lives.

One of the accused, Susanna Martin, was reported to have threatened to send a she-devil to attack a man. The following night, the man woke to find a cat-shaped demon sneaking through his window. The demon seized him by the throat and would, he claimed, have murdered him if he had not cried out, 'Avoid, thou She-Devil! In the name of God the Father, the Son, and the Holy Ghost, Avoid!'

At the same trial, many of the accused were forced into confessions. One claimed to have met the Devil in the shape of a cat; another that she overheard two cats large as dogs talking; yet another maintained that a cat, calling itself 'the prince of the air' (the Devil), had promised wealth in exchange for fealty.

Both an obsession with unearthing witches and a linking of witches with cats are evident in this story, an African American tale whose roots stretch back to Europe and the sixteenth century.

In the olden days there was a house-girl for a family of slave owners. The family had made a fortune from sheep farming.

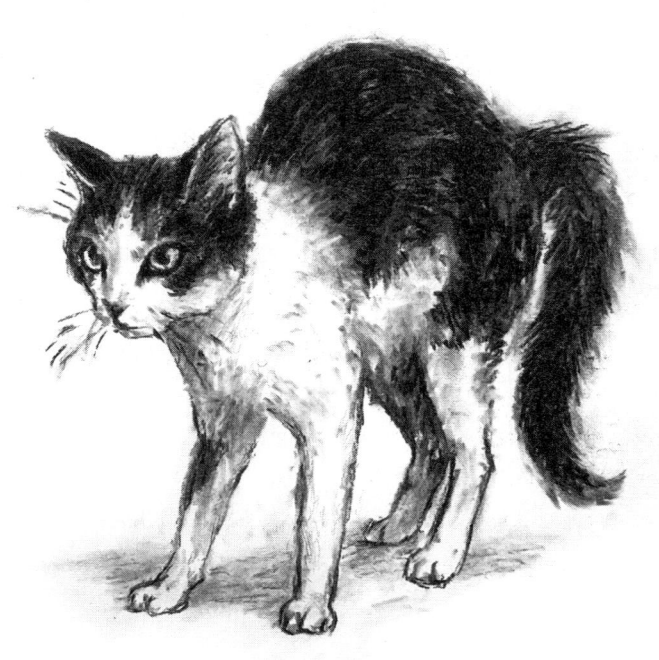

The Malevolent Cat

Their flock was so large, in fact, that there was too much wool for their barns, so they stored great mounds of the stuff in the attic.

One morning it was discovered that some wool was missing. The master – as the slave owner was known – was enraged. Missing wool meant missing money, and that was all he cared about. From then on, he checked the wool each morning, and each morning the pile had shrunk a little more, growing smaller and smaller and smaller.

The master decided that a thief was stealing his wool. He blamed the house-girl, for she often went into the attic to clean. Though she swore that she was innocent, the cruel master did not believe her. He gave her a horrible whipping, leaving her back bloody and scarred.

As the poor girl tended her wounds, she wondered who the real thief could be. She remembered that she had often seen a ginger cat sitting among the wool.

'Perhaps the cat is swiping the wool,' she thought. Taking a knife, she went up to the attic to investigate. Sure enough, she found the cat dozing in the corner.

'I'll cut off its head,' the girl decided. 'That will stop it thieving – and pay it back for my whipping.'

She edged towards the cat and grabbed it by the back paw. Raising her knife high, she aimed a blow at the animal's neck. The cat, however, wriggled and writhed, hissing and scratching, trying to break free. When the girl brought down the knife, she missed her target. Instead, it struck the animal's front paw, slicing

The Cat-Witch

it clean off. Letting out a hideous howl, the cat fled down the stairs and out of the front door.

The girl picked up the paw. To her horror, the bloody appendage turned into a human hand. Now she understood: a witch had changed herself into a cat.

Immediately, she rushed downstairs and showed the hand to her mistress, who showed the master, who showed the neighbours, who told the whole town. And, like that, a witch-hunt began, for witches were hated and feared. The townsfolk searched for a woman with a missing hand; that woman, they knew, would be the witch.

As it happened, a rich merchant had recently moved to the town with his beautiful red-haired wife. The couple had seemed perfectly ordinary – boring, even. But that morning, to the husband's shock, his wife had appeared at breakfast with only one hand. And, later, when rumours of the cat-witch reached his ears, he knew that his wife was guilty.

The man loved his wife very much. But he lacked the courage to live with a witch. In despair, he confessed his suspicions to his neighbours. Soon a mob formed. Kicking down the front door, they dragged the woman, fighting and screaming, from the house and out into the town square.

And, as was done to witches in those days, they tied her to a stake and set her on fire and burned her until she was dead.

The Nunda, Eater of People

· Swahili ·

In this Swahili tale, the Nunda is a monstrous cat with an equally monstrous appetite. It is an example of a 'swallowing monster' – a creature not only capable of eating anything, but that grows larger with each new meal. In this case, it swells from a seemingly normal cat to a beast terrorising a country. Such creatures recur throughout African folklore, including the Khanyapa, a shapeless monster of the Basotho people, and the Zulu's Usiququmadevu, a female monster who can devour whole villages in a single mouthful.

In some tales, the Nunda, also known as the Mngwa ('strange one'), is a therianthrope – that is, a human capable of shapeshifting into an animal. However, though its description varies, it is most often depicted as a giant cat. In Africa, a land of actual deadly cats, it is natural to find legends of monstrous felines.

A long time ago there was a sultan with seven sons. He loved the eldest six with his whole heart. But the youngest son was so sensitive and odd that the sultan did not love him one bit.

Even more than his six eldest sons, however, the sultan loved his pleasure garden. It was his pride and joy, full of every variety of fruit and flower. His favourite was a large date tree in the centre of the courtyard.

The Nunda, Eater of People

One day, to the sultan's delight, the date tree bore fruit. He instructed his eldest son to stand guard, lest anyone should steal a single date. The eldest son, desperate to protect the tree and impress his father, was worried that he'd fall asleep. So, he ordered his servants to beat their drums through the night, hoping this would help him stay awake. His ploy, however, proved unsuccessful, for the servants found the drumming tiring, and the stress of waiting was draining. Near dawn, the prince and his exhausted men fell into a deep slumber beneath the tree.

While they slept, a bird flew to the tree. It gobbled one date after another, until none were left.

The sultan was livid. 'You have failed as a son,' he whispered (which was far scarier than him shouting). 'Leave and never come back.'

After that, the tree bore fruit each year and, each year, the sultan sent a son to guard it. The second son took a platoon of soldiers; the third threw a party with jugglers; the fourth lit a raging bonfire; the fifth brought a lion on a leash; the sixth beat himself with sticks – anything that might help them stay awake and stop the bird.

Not one of them succeeded, however. The sons kept falling asleep, the bird kept stealing the dates, and the sultan kept banishing his sons from the palace.

Finally, only the youngest son – the odd, unloved son – remained. Begging an audience with his father, he offered to protect the date tree.

The sultan pulled a face. 'You? Guard the tree? Why, six brave sons have failed!' he said bitterly. 'What's the point of sending a good-for-nothing like you?'

But the sultan's wife convinced him, saying, 'Why must you be so cruel, my dear? Anyway, we have no dates now, so what have we to lose?'

And so the boy was permitted to guard the tree. But he didn't take soldiers or servants. He didn't take jugglers or lions or beating sticks. He simply leant his back against the trunk and dozed until midnight, then rose and hid in the bushes. Every time his eyes grew heavy, he sprinkled a pinch of sand in his mouth, and that stopped him dozing.

At dawn, the bird appeared. It hopped towards the tree, stealthy as a burglar breaking into a bank.

Then – crash! – the boy bolted from the bushes and tackled the bird. The thief was ferociously strong, however, and flew into the air, lifting the lad with him. Together they soared over the land. Petrified, the boy held on for dear life, gripping so tightly that his fingers cramped and his arms turned to jelly. But he never let go.

'Turn around!' yelled the boy.

'No!' squawked the bird.

'I'm taking you home!'

'Impossible!'

'Go back!'

'Never!'

But eventually the bird was too weary to continue. It gave in, crying, 'OK, OK, OK! I'll take you back!'

'And you won't eat the dates again?' demanded the boy.

'I promise – I won't eat the dates again!' it said. 'Just get your hands off me!'

Then it turned around and took the boy home.

The next morning, when he saw the dates on the tree, the sultan was in raptures.

'My dearest son!' he cried, hugging the boy. 'You are worth more than the other six put together. I'm *glad* they're banished!'

But the lad was a good brother. On bended knee, he persuaded his father to let the other sons return to the palace.

The sultan was overjoyed. Not only was his beloved date tree safe, but his family had been made whole once more. To celebrate, the sultan decided to buy a cat as a reminder of the happy day. A black-and-white kitten, it was a tiny creature, small enough to rest on the palm of the sultan's hand. He loved this kitten dearly – for beneath his stern exterior the sultan had a tender heart – and would not allow it to be trained or disciplined in any way. It had the run of the palace and the pleasure garden, and no one dared deny it anything: the cooks let it steal from the kitchens; the maids allowed it to knock vases off the mantelpieces; and the gardeners watched on as it made mischief in the flowerbeds.

But the tiny creature did not stay tiny for long. It simply grew and grew. And as it grew, it ate more and more. It ate bread and rice and porridge and stew. It ate cake and chocolate, caramel and tarts. But the sultan loved the cat and refused to have it punished.

'It is *my* cat,' he said, 'and that is *my* food. It may eat it if it wishes.'

Then the cat ate mice and dogs and goats and fowl. It ate donkeys and horses, cows and camels. But still the sultan loved the cat and refused to have it punished.

'It is *my* cat,' he said, 'and they are *my* animals. It may eat them if it wishes.'

Then the cat ate a baby. After the baby it ate a child. And after the child it ate an adult.

But even then, the sultan *still* refused to have it punished.

'It is *my* cat,' he said, 'and they are *my* people. It may eat them if it wishes.'

Then, to the sultan's great disappointment, the cat ran away. Sometimes it lived in the town and ate its fill of townsfolk. Sometimes it lived in the country and dined on the countryfolk. Usually, though, it lived in a copse by the road, from where it could catch passing prey. It killed so many travellers it came to be feared throughout the realm.

But the sultan refused to believe the beast could be *his* cat.

'No, no,' he said, 'it can't be *my* cat. He's a good boy – the very best! He wouldn't hurt a fly!'

'My dear, you know that's not *quite* true,' said his wife gently. 'He did, after all, eat that baby. And that child. And that adult.'

The Nunda, Eater of People

'Yes, well,' blustered the sultan, 'everyone gets peckish sometimes, don't they?'

'Of course, my dear. But perhaps we should send some soldiers to catch him,' suggested the queen. 'In case he gets peckish again?'

'Absolutely not!' shouted the sultan. 'If this creature *is* my cat, then no one shall hurt a hair on its little head! Ever! On pain of death!'

A few days later, the sultan decided to inspect his land. He asked his sons to accompany him. At first, all was well. But when they reached the copse, they were startled by a mighty roar. A monstrous creature shot out from the trees. It was the cat, now grown to a colossal size – larger than any lion or tiger. Humungous and ferocious, its white-furred breast was stained with blood, and its fangs were like knives glistening in its jaws.

It sent a thrill of terror down the spines of all who saw it – even the sultan. Snarling, growling, the beast pounced, devouring the three eldest sons. Then it sloped back into the trees.

'My boys!' cried the sultan, sinking to his knees. 'My cat killed my boys! It is no longer a cat of mine! No, now it is the Nunda, eater of people!'

And the sultan broke into deep, painful sobs.

The youngest son was grief-stricken at the loss of his brothers. But he was also enraged. Grabbing his spear, he chased after the cat, tracking it through grasslands and deserts, forests and mountains. After a long chase, he came to the top of a tall peak. From there he could see across the land. At the foot of the mountain, he spied the Nunda.

The boy made his way down the slope. Near the bottom was overgrown brush, full of thorny branches and tangled trees. The lad crawled through the briars and brambles. Soon, his hands were bloody and knees were sore. But, finally, he reached the lair where the cat slept.

Then, when he was close enough, the boy rose and took aim. He threw his spear, piercing the demon cat through the heart.

The Nunda, eater of people, was dead.

In the morning, he dragged the cat's corpse back to the palace. Everyone, from sultan to servant, was jubilant, for the land was finally rid of the beast.

And the next time the sultan wanted a pet he got a dog instead.

7

The Unfortunate Cat

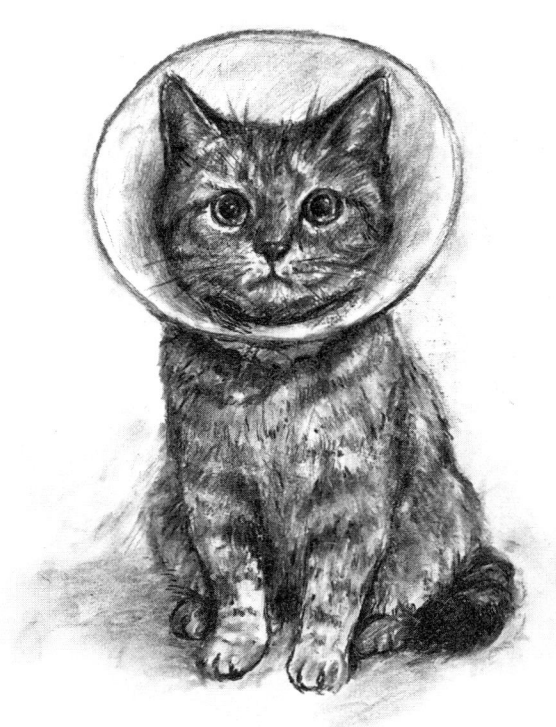

Cats are utterly ridiculous. They can flit from being gods and goddesses, creatures of smoke and shadows, to a puzzled pet with a face stuck in a yoghurt pot. These animals, so dignified, so composed, are capable of forgetting how to use the cat flap or trapping themselves in cardboard boxes; of fighting their own reflections or scrabbling (unsuccessfully) to climb out of baths.

And when they do come a cropper, it is a delight to see the consternation on their faces, or to witness their attempts to feign unruffled indifference. Cats are always too sure of their superiority to admit that anything could have been *their* fault.

The zaniness of cats may be the consequence of predatory behaviour. When kittens, they play and explore, fight and chase, in order to hone their hunting skills. As they age, they slow down and mellow, but they never completely lose this instinct. Even an elderly cat may suddenly feel the impulse to chase a crumpled piece of wrapping paper or pounce on a pair of slippers. And, of course, the more they play, and the more they lose themselves in a game, the more likely they are to find themselves in an undignified position: perched on top of a door, say, or marooned in the branches of a tree.

They may also be led into unfortunate circumstances by their famed curiosity. Seemingly, they cannot see a box or a bag, a nook or a cranny, without wishing to squeeze inside. Getting out, however, is not always so easy. They are constantly exploring the world, evaluating new objects, finding new places. To do this, they pat things, they bat things, they lick and they sniff, they crawl and climb and scratch. Like playing, curiosity is a natural instinct. It is how they appraise their surroundings, learning what is safe and what is dangerous.

This vigilance is important for cats. As mesopredators – that is, they are both hunters and hunted – they are positioned, rather uncomfortably, in the middle of the food chain. They must remain alert for opportunities to eat, but also constantly look over their shoulders, making sure they are not eaten. Consequently, they are obliged to be ever inquisitive. This curiosity may help to keep them alive (and well fed), but it also ensures that they blunder into situations they have no place to be in.

And so cats are both the cleverest of animals, and the most foolish; models of sophistication, and complete klutzes. Often, the cats in these stories are the creators of their own misfortune. As tricksters, they are never without a cunning plan up their sleeves. But while these ploys may succeed, they are often foiled. Other times, the cats themselves fall victim to a trick – for cats in stories, like cats in real life, are rarely quite as smart as they believe themselves to be. In the Indian tale 'The Story of a Cat, a Mouse, a Lizard and an Owl', the cat proves gullible, fooled by the quick-thinking mouse. In 'The Two Cats', an Arabic tale, the poor cat is forced by his hunger to take unwise risks – with unhappy consequences. And, though they are frequently hunting for food in stories, cats can also be the hunted, as in 'The Cat and the Crow', a tale from *One Thousand and One Nights*.

However, this penchant for the absurd, this tendency to be luckless, is not an unappealing quality in cats. Quite the opposite.

The lucklessness undercuts the grander side of the cat: the side that is elegant and superior, the side worshipped as gods. In doing so, it makes them softer and more approachable – and more relatable. For, while we shall never understand what it is to be a revered deity, we all know what it is to make a fool of ourselves.

Cats are lovable for many reasons. But they are never more heart-meltingly charming than when embarrassing themselves.

The Two Cats

· Arabic ·

Cats are admired in Islamic cultures. Unlike many animals, such as dogs, cats are respected for their cleanliness, for, as the prophet Muhammad said, 'Cats are not impure, as they meander around you.' Consequently, they are ruled ritually clean under Islamic law, being permitted to roam houses, businesses and even mosques.

According to some legends, Muhammad himself had a beloved cat named Muezza. Muhammad would hold the cat in his arms while preaching and would use water Muezza had drunk from to perform his ablutions. Once he even cut off the sleeve from his prayer robe rather than disturb his cat, who had fallen asleep on the garment. These stories go some way to explaining the honoured place the cat has in Islam.

Not that this cultural acceptance helps the poor cat in this Arabic folk tale. As so often, the cat is led by its appetite, which proves its downfall.

An old woman owned a cat made miserable for want of food. The woman was kind, and loved her cat dearly, but they were so poor she could barely afford to feed it. Though she shared all that she had, there was rarely more than a bit of bread or a bowl of rice to go round, and often there was nothing at all. The cat grew thin, its tabby fur patchy, its eyes dull.

The Unfortunate Cat

'We can't go on like this!' grumbled the cat one evening, as they sat in their little hut. 'Nothing for lunch! Nothing for dinner! I'm wasting away!'

'Now, now, it's not all bad. We should try to appreciate what we have,' the old woman counselled.

'But we don't have anything,' muttered the cat. 'That's the problem.'

The old woman smiled. 'Well, I think we have plenty,' she said, giving the cat a stroke. 'After all, we have our home. And we have each other.'

'Fat lot of good that does us!' thought the cat bitterly, listening to the gurgles in its tummy.

The next morning, half starved, the cat managed to catch a mouse. It eked out the meal for a whole week, enjoying every last nibble and bite. But soon it was starving again. Lying on the roof of the hut, brooding on its empty belly, it saw another cat. A beautiful Siamese with bright blue eyes, it was sunning itself on a nearby wall. Unlike the poor cat, which was all skin and bones, this cat was plump and healthy.

'Friend!' called the poor cat. 'Tell me your secret! How are you so sleek and shiny, while I'm so scrawny I can barely lift my head?'

'It's simple. I'm crumb-eater for the sultan,' the rich cat explained proudly. 'His meals are so extravagant there's always plenty to spare. All I do is take my pick from what's left of his feasts.'

The poor cat felt glummer than ever. 'It's all right for some!

You're tucking into royal feasts, while I'm lucky if I get a measly mouse. Most days I have nothing at all!'

'Well, that explains why you're such a pathetic creature,' said the rich cat, preening itself. 'Frankly, I am embarrassed to be seen with you.'

'I know, I know,' cringed the other. 'But, friend, perhaps you could take me to the palace? If I had a proper meal or two, I'd soon look better.'

The rich cat, though snooty, was not a bad sort deep down. He agreed to accompany the poor cat to the palace the next day.

That night, the poor cat told the old lady what had happened.

The woman was worried. 'Be careful now,' she warned. 'Greed is dangerous; it can make folk do all manner of silly things. Sometimes you don't know what you have until it's gone.'

But it was too late. Plates of imaginary food drifted before the cat's eyes – lamb and couscous, dates and honey. Nothing, now, could prevent it from attending the sultan's breakfast.

The next day, the two cats set off for the palace. But the poor cat, weak with hunger, hobbled so slowly the pair were late.

As it happened, earlier that morning, a crowd of cats had swarmed the dining hall. They had caused such a disturbance that the guards had chased them away. Livid, the sultan had ordered his archers to shoot the next creature who tried to steal his food.

The poor cat was unaware of this, of course. So, seeing the table laden with delicious dishes, it leapt up and tore into a tender piece of chicken. No sooner did it taste the food in its mouth, however, than an arrow pierced its side. Moaning in pain, the cat crawled away, leaving a trail of blood behind it.

'I don't need feasts and palaces,' it sobbed. 'Just give me my mistress and my safe old hut. Just give me life.'

Slowly, painfully, the cat made its way home to the kind old woman. She been right, the cat realised. You don't know what you have until it's gone.

'If I survive,' the cat thought, 'I'll never again take what I have for granted. I'll appreciate all the good things in life, whether they be big or small!'

And, from that day forth, that's just what the cat did.

The Story of a Cat, a Mouse, a Lizard and an Owl

· Indian ·

Cats do not play a large part in Indian folklore, nor are they common as pets in the country. This is due largely to their association with sorcery and their reputation for deviousness, which has led them to being considered bad omens.

They do occasionally feature in Hindu mythology: Shashthi, the goddess of fertility and the protector of children, rides upon a cat; and the deity Kaumari also uses a cat as a mount. However, in the instances when they feature in tales and legends, it is usually to illustrate their slippery natures.

This story is an ancient one, with roots stretching back to the Mahabharata, *a Sanskrit epic compiled between the third and fourth century* BCE. *A version also features in the eleventh-century* Kathasaritsagara, *a collection of legends retold by the Kashmiri writer Somadeva.*

A cat, a mouse, a lizard and an owl lived in a banyan tree. The cat lived in a hole in the trunk. The owl had a nest at the crown. The lizard lazed upon a branch. And the mouse slept in the thick, twisted roots at the bottom. But it was so scared of the cat and the owl that it rarely had a good night's rest.

The Unfortunate Cat

One evening, the mouse took a walk in a field. The cat saw it go and, feeling peckish, set off after it. The cat was arrogant, however, and paid no attention to the tracks it made. It stomped through the barley, leaving a path in its wake.

A hunter spotted the trail. 'A cat?' he said, studying the pawprints. 'It's been many a moon since I bagged one of those.'

And he laid a rope trap.

Not long after, the mouse scampered past. It had heard the cat following and knew it had to return home to safety. Now it hurried and scurried, winding and weaving, fleeing the claws of the cat. The cat was inches away, and just about to pounce, when it stepped in the trap. Snap! It was caught tight and couldn't budge.

'Aha!' cried the mouse. 'Serves you right!'

But the little fellow shouted so loudly it drew the attention of the owl. Now the bird circled in the moonlight, waiting for the perfect moment to swoop.

'I'm in trouble now!' realised the mouse. 'If I run *that* way, the owl will catch me; but if I run *this* way, I'll end up in the cat's jaws.'

Then it had an excellent idea. 'If I stay near the cat, the owl won't swoop; it's nearly as scared of the cat as I am. If I can survive until morning, when the owl goes to bed, I might have a chance.'

It turned to the cat. 'Dear Puss,' it said. 'I propose a truce. If you promise not to eat me, I'll promise to save you from the trap.'

Now, the cat was a proud creature, as all cats are; it was

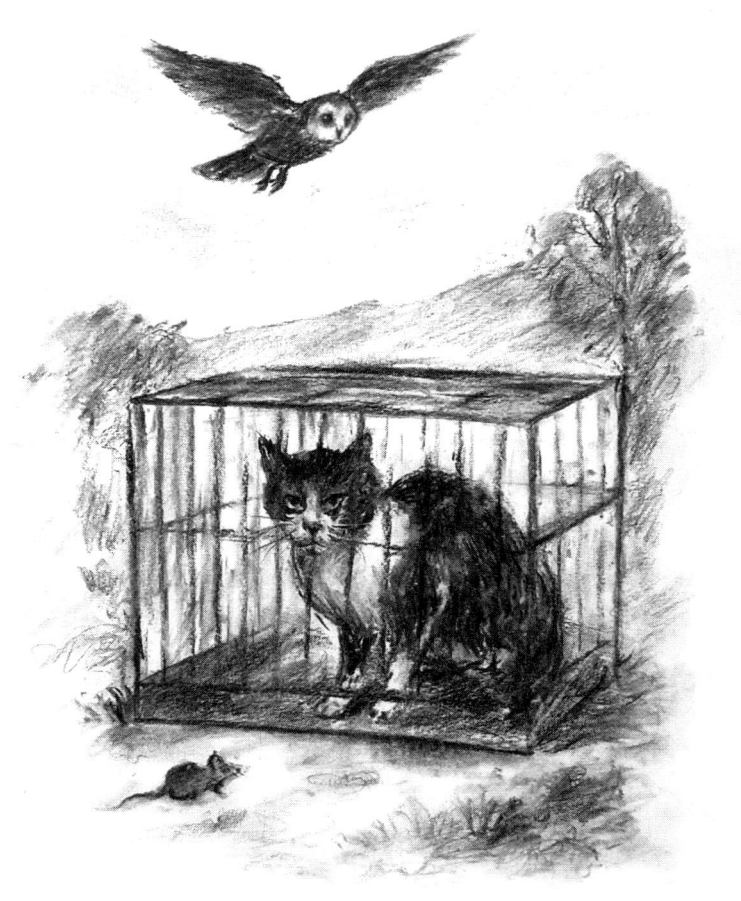

loath to accept the mouse's help. But it had little choice: if it remained trapped until the hunter returned then it was as good as dead. So, with claws crossed behind its back, it swore to not hurt the mouse.

The mouse, of course, was too smart to trust the cat. So, it only *pretended* to gnaw at the rope that bound the cat.

'Nearly there . . .' it lied.

'One minute . . .' it fibbed.

'Any second now . . .' it faked.

And in this manner, the mouse bluffed the cat all night long.

At dawn the hunter tramped across the field. The cat saw him coming and panicked. 'Mouse, I beg you!' it squealed. 'The hunter is here – please let me out!'

And the mouse (keeping its promise) snipped at the rope with its teeth. The cat was free. It fled from the hunter one way; the mouse fled from the cat the other; the owl, fed up of waiting, had already gone home for a nap.

The next day, the cat sat outside the mouse's den. It realised it had been played for a fool and was fuming. 'Darling Mouse,' it purred. 'Come out, I want to thank you for last night. Why don't you come round for dinner?'

'It's OK,' squeaked the mouse – knowing *it* was the dinner the cat would serve. 'I haven't any appetite.'

The cat waited. And it waited and waited and waited some more. But the sensible mouse never strayed from its hole.

So the cat grew bored, gave up, and ate the lizard instead.

And, later, the mouse was killed by the owl.

The Lion and the Cat

· Native American ·

Domestic cats are not native to North America, arriving only in the 1600s with European colonists. Consequently, they play little part in traditional Native American tales. The various wildcats and large cats of North America, however, including bobcats, lynxes and pumas, were important folkloric figures, often symbolising independence and intuition.

The cat in this Native American tale, therefore, is probably a wildcat. Nevertheless, it displays many of the recognisable features of its domesticated cousin. Additionally, since there are no lions in the New World, the lion in the story must, in fact, be a cougar (also known as a puma or a mountain lion).

Once there was a lion who lived with a cat. The lion was a magnificent hunter, strong and fast. But the cat, though small, boasted courage and brains. What's more, he possessed a golden ball of tremendous power. Bright as the sun, the magical ball ensured that no harm could come to the cat while he owned it. So, naturally, he kept it safe, tucked in the thick fur around his neck.

One morning the lion and the cat went out to hunt.

'Right,' said the cat, as they set off across the meadow, 'listen up. I know where some deer are grazing. We'll catch two – but we'll only eat one. The other we'll keep alive, as I have a fancy to ride it like a horse.'

The Unfortunate Cat

The lion shot his friend a funny look. 'What?' he said.

'You heard. I really fancy riding a deer like a horse,' repeated the cat. 'I think it'll be fun.'

The lion shrugged. 'Well, OK, as long as I get to eat one,' he said. 'I'm famished!'

The pair continued through the meadow. It was a sunny day. Flowers bloomed all around them, blue and pink and yellow. The friends – one little, one large – trotted along quietly. Coming to a pebbly stream, they splashed through the cold water to the other side. After shaking themselves dry, they made their way to a small wood.

As they reached the trees, however, the lion suddenly stopped in its tracks.

'There's a bear in that tree,' worried the lion. 'He'll jump on me when we pass. Cat, *please* save me from his big fierce teeth!'

Taking out the golden ball, the cat made a wish: 'Die, bear, die!'

And the bear dropped from the tree with a thud. They didn't eat the bear, however, as the lion was too scared – even when the bear was dead.

The lion and the cat came to a field of tall grass, swaying gently in the breeze.

'There's a snake in that grass,' fretted the lion. 'He'll strike at my ankles when we pass. Cat, *please* save me from his nasty venom!'

Taking out the golden ball, the cat made a wish: 'Die, snake, die!'

The Lion and the Cat

And the snake, writhing in pain, twisted itself into a knot and perished. They didn't eat the snake, however, as neither of them enjoyed the taste.

Then the lion and the cat came to a hill where a herd of deer was grazing.

'Catch us two deer,' the cat told his friend. 'But remember: kill one, then keep the other alive, for I'd like to ride it like a horse.'

The cat went home and waited for the lion.

'Did you catch the deer?' he asked when the lion returned. 'Did you bring one dead and one alive?'

'Well, yes and no,' replied the lion, picking a morsel of deer from his teeth. 'By the time I got my claws on them I didn't have the energy to lug them here. So I ate them both.'

The cat was angry and went to bed in a thunderous mood. Not only was he hungry, but his heart had been set on riding the deer like a horse.

The next day the cat, still grumpy, refused to hunt. The lion, meanwhile, was too scared to leave the hut without him. This argument went on for days, and they both grew ravenous, for they had no food to eat.

'I wish I had the golden ball,' thought the lion. 'Then I wouldn't need the cat to help me catch a tasty lunch.'

The lion decided to steal the ball.

'Cat, how about a game of catch?' he suggested, trying to be crafty. 'We could use your golden ball.'

The cat shook his head. 'I don't care for catch,' he sulked.

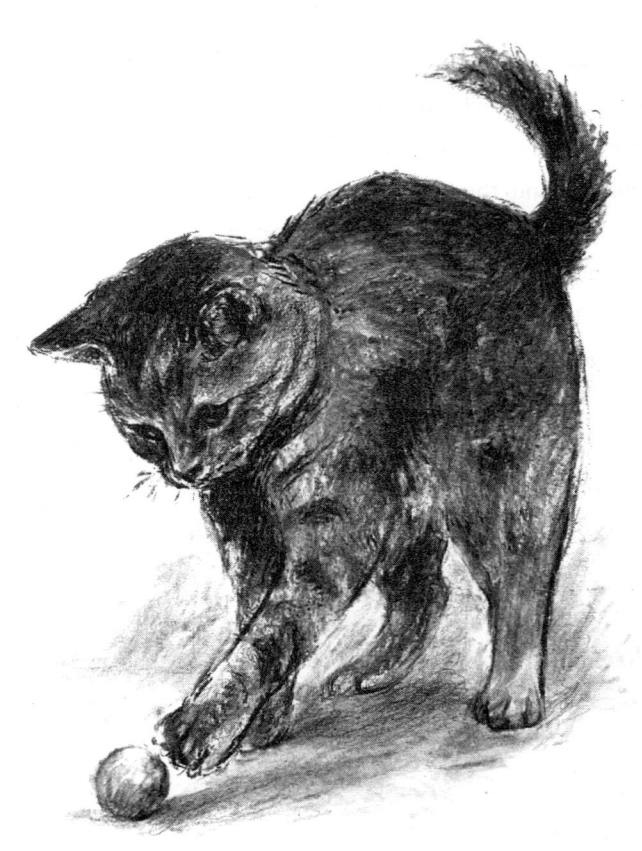

'Perhaps I could borrow it?' asked the lion. 'I'll play on my own.'

'No. You'll lose it in the bushes,' said the cat. 'Your paws are too big and clumsy.'

But the lion nagged and badgered and pleaded and pestered until, finally, the cat threw him the ball. And no sooner did the lion have it in his paws than he dashed outside and tossed the ball high into the air – so high he couldn't see where it had flown.

'You dolt!' spat the cat. 'We must find it! We must find the ball!'

They searched all day and all night, but they never found the golden ball.

The cat was incensed; he could no longer live under the same roof as the lion. He left, travelling far and wide, and everywhere he went he sought his golden ball.

One day he came to a great river at the base of a mountain. The ground was soggy, for the river had burst its banks, and the cat climbed into a tree to stop his paws from getting damp. There, to his glee, he saw his golden ball balancing on a branch.

'At last!' he cried, stretching for it. 'My golden ball!'

But try as he might, it was just out of reach, and when he tried to crawl closer, the branch began to creak and crack, for it was too thin to bear his weight. The cat did not give up. He climbed to a higher, thicker branch and, dangling from it with his paws, he knocked the ball to the ground with a swish of his tail. He dashed down the tree and, delirious, tucked the ball in the thick fur at his neck.

The Unfortunate Cat

The cat decided to cross the river. But it was too wide to swim and there were no boats to be found. Spotting two women playing on the other bank, the cat jumped up and down, waving his arms, hoping to catch their attention. But as he did so, the ball fell from his fur and splashed into the river.

'No!' shrieked the cat. 'Not again!'

He watched, horrified, as the ball floated across the river and nestled in the reeds. The women fished it from the water. It was the most dazzling object they had ever seen. Tossing it to and fro, they marvelled at the sunlight playing on its surface. When night fell, they locked it in the cupboard by their bed.

The next morning, they rose early and rushed to the cupboard, too excited to wait. Imagine their astonishment, then, when instead of a golden ball they saw a lovely young man, tall and handsome!

He bowed to them in gratitude and said, 'Many years ago, a wicked spirit turned me into a ball. The only way to return to my human form was for two women to take me to their home. But I fell into the paws of a cat, who shunned humans and kept to the forests and the mountains. Then the lion threw me in the air and I escaped. When I fell in the river and saw the two of you, I knew my chance had arrived. If you ever need my help, climb to the top of the mountain and knock three times on the iron door. At that time, I will return.'

Then he left and the two ladies wept most bitterly – but whether for the loss of a golden ball or a handsome young man, I couldn't possibly say.

The Cat and the Crow

· Arabic ·

This is a story from One Thousand and One Nights, *a huge compendium of tales that draws from the traditions of Arabian and Persian literature and features stories from all over the Islamic world. Each night, Scheherazade spins a yarn to King Shahryar, hoping to make her stories so compelling that the monarch will wish to continue listening – and so will not behead her in the morning.*

One night, the king requests a tale of the 'beauty of true friendship'. Scheherazade recounts a story of an unfortunate cat, not observant or fast enough to save itself, who is rescued by the courage and quick thinking of its friend, the crow.

In reality, cats and crows are far from allies. Cats will hunt crows, despite their large size, and crows are more than capable of fighting back. Among the cleverest of birds, there is evidence they take pre-emptive defensive measures, with flocks witnessed attacking cats. What is more, they seem to enjoy instigating cat fights by nipping the tails of cats, provoking them into scrapping with any cats nearby. This may be to protect themselves, or it may simply be from a sense of mischief.

A cat and a crow were the best of friends.

They made a good team: from a tree-top perch or high in the sky, the crow spotted prey for them to catch; while the cat, bigger

The Unfortunate Cat

and stronger, hunted creatures the bird could never bag on its own. And whatever they caught they shared, without quibbling or squabbling. But, more than this, they were all that friends should be, for they made each other laugh, and offered support in times of need, and each found the long cold nights in the forest a little shorter, a little warmer because of the other.

One day, as they chatted in the shade of a tree, a leopard prowled their way, hoping to have them for supper. It was so stealthy and sly, they didn't know the danger until it was almost too late.

The crow fluttered up into the safety of the canopy. But the hapless cat was stranded at the bottom.

'Crow!' it yowled. 'Save me, please!'

Now, the crow was not the type to abandon its friends. It was desperate to rescue the cat. So, it flew into the sky and circled the forest until it spied a hunter and his dogs.

'*Kraak! Kraak!*' the crow cawed, trying to get their attention.

Then, once spotted, the bird flew dangerously low, its belly tickled by the tips of the grass, the angry hounds snapping at its tail. In this way, the crow steered them back to the leopard and the cat.

'What took you so long?' cried the cat. 'I'm nearly a goner here!'

The cat was right. The crow wasn't a moment too soon, for the leopard was about to lunge. However, the dogs made such a hullaballoo – howling and growling – that the leopard was terrified. It skulked back into the heart of the forest, away from the hounds' sharp teeth.

And the cat and the crow were safe and sound and better friends than ever.

Sources

'When the Cat Ruled the World': Andrew Anderson, *The Magic of Cats* (Moon Books, 2023); Natalie Boris, *Cat Gods, Goddesses, Deities, and Demons* (Running Press, 2025)

'The Cat Who Came Indoors': Hugh Tracey, *The Lion on the Path and Other African Stories* (Frederick A. Praeger, 1968)

'The Cat's Purr': Ashley Bryan, *The Cat's Purr* (Atheneum, 1985); Elsie Clews Parsons, 'Why Cat Eats Rat', *Folklore of the Antilles*, vol. 2 (The American Folk-Lore Society, 1936)

'Why Cats Always Wash after Eating': Jean de Bosschère, *Beasts & Men: Folk Tales Collected in Flanders* (W. Heinemann, 1918)

'Why the Dog Hates the Cat': Norman Hinsdale Pitman, 'The Golden Beetle', *A Chinese Wonder Book* (E. P. Dutton & Co., 1919)

'How the Manx Cat Lost Its Tail': Sophia Morrison, *Manx Fairy Tales* (David Nutt, 1911)

'Why the Cat Kills Rats': Elphinstone Dayrell, *Folk Stories from Southern Nigeria, West Africa* (Longmans, Green & Co., 1910)

'The Little White Cat': Edmund Leamy, *Irish Fairy Tales* (M. H. Gill, 1906)

'The Colony of Cats': Andrew Lang, *The Crimson Fairy Book* (Longmans, Green & Co., 1903)

'The White Cat': Madame d'Aulnoy, *The Fairy Tales of Madame d'Aulnoy* (London, Lawrence and Bullen, 1892); Andrew Lang, *The Blue Fairy Book* (Longmans, Green & Co., 1889)

'The Bank Cat': Atha Westbury, *Australian Fairy Tales* (Ward, Lock, & Co., 1897)

The Cat's Tales

'Johnny Reed's Cat': Charles John Tibbits, *Folk-Lore and Legends: English* (W. W. Gibbings, 1890); Kathleen Hersom, *Johnny Reed's Cat and Other Northern Tales* (A. & C. Black, 1987)

'Kisa the Cat': Andrew Lang, *The Brown Fairy Book* (Longmans, Green & Co., 1904)

'The Poor Miller's Boy and the Cat': Jacob and Wilhelm Grimm, *Grimms' Fairy Tales* (Routledge & Kegan Paul, 1948)

'The Boy Who Drew Cats': Lafcadio Hearn et al., *Japanese Fairy Tales* (Boni and Liveright, 1918)

'The Enchanted Cat': Baroness Orczy, *The Enchanted Cat* (Dean and Wolf, 1895)

'Puss in Boots': Charles Perrault, *Perrault's Fairy Tales* (Jonathan Cape, 1967)

'Cat and Mouse in Partnership': Jacob and Wilhelm Grimm, *Grimms' Fairy Tales* (Routledge & Kegan Paul, 1948)

'The Cat and the Birds', *Aesop's Fables* (Wordsworth Editions, 1994)

'The Clever Cat': Andrew Lang, *The Orange Fairy Book* (Longmans, Green & Co., 1906)

'The Cat and the Mice': W. F. O'Connor, *Folk Tales from Tibet* (Hurst and Blackett, 1906)

'The Fox and the Cat': *Aesop's Fables* (Wordsworth Editions, 1994); Jacob and Wilhelm Grimm, *Grimms' Fairy Tales* (Routledge & Kegan Paul, 1948)

'Dick Whittington and His Cat': Andrew Lang, *The Blue Fairy Book* (Longmans, Green & Co., 1889); Joseph Jacobs, *English Fairy Tales* (David Nutt, 1890)

'The Cottager and His Cat': Andrew Lang, *The Crimson Fairy Book* (Longmans, Green & Co., 1903)

'The Cat's Elopement': Andrew Lang, *The Pink Fairy Book* (Longmans, Green & Co., 1897)

'Venus and the Cat', *Aesop's Fables* (Wordsworth Editions, 1994)

'Silvershod': *The Fairy Tale Book*, trans. Marie Ponsot (Golden Books Publishing/Simon & Schuster, 1958)

Sources

'The Greedy Cat': *Tales from the Fjeld, A Series of Popular Tales from the Norse of P. Ch. Asbjørnsen*, trans. Sir George Dasent (G. P. Putnam's Sons, 1917)

'Catafay and the Fox': Alexander Afanasiev, 'Liza the Fox and Catafay the Cat', *The Magic Ring: Russian Folk Tales* (Raduga Publishers, 1985); James Riordan, 'Liza the Fox and Catafay the Cat', *Tales from Central Russia: Russian Tales – Book One* (Harmondsworth, 1976)

'The Cat and the Cock': *Aesop's Fables* (Wordsworth Editions, 1994)

'The Black Cat': Pinhas Sadeh, *Jewish Folktales* (Anchor Books/Doubleday, 1989)

'King Arthur and the Cat': Lady Jane Wilde, *Ancient Legends, Mystic Charms and Superstitions of Ireland* (Ticknor & Co., 1887); Katharine M. Briggs, *Nine Lives: Cats in Folklore* (Routledge & Kegan Paul, 1980)

'The Demon Cat': Lady Jane Wilde, *Ancient Legends, Mystic Charms and Superstitions of Ireland* (Ticknor & Co., 1887)

'The Cat Witches': W. Jenkyn Thomas, *The Welsh Fairy Book* (T. Fisher Unwin, 1907)

'The Cat-Witch': Angela Carter (ed.), *The Virago Book of Fairy Tales* (Virago Press, 1990)

'The Nunda, Eater of People': Edward Steere, *Swahili Tales, as Told by Natives of Zanzibar* (Bell & Daldy, 1870); Andrew Lang, *The Violet Fairy Book* (Longmans, Green & Co., 1901)

'The Two Cats': Charles John Tibbits, *Folk-Lore and Legends: Oriental* (W. W. Gibbings, 1889)

'The Story of a Cat, a Mouse, a Lizard and an Owl': *Hindu Tales from the Sanskrit*, trans. S. M. Mitra (Macmillan and Co., 1919)

'The Lion and the Cat': Andrew Lang, *The Brown Fairy Book* (Longmans, Green & Co., 1904)

'The Cat and the Crow', *The Book of the Thousand Nights and One Night*, vol. 3, trans. John Payne (London, for the Villon Society by private subscription, 1901)

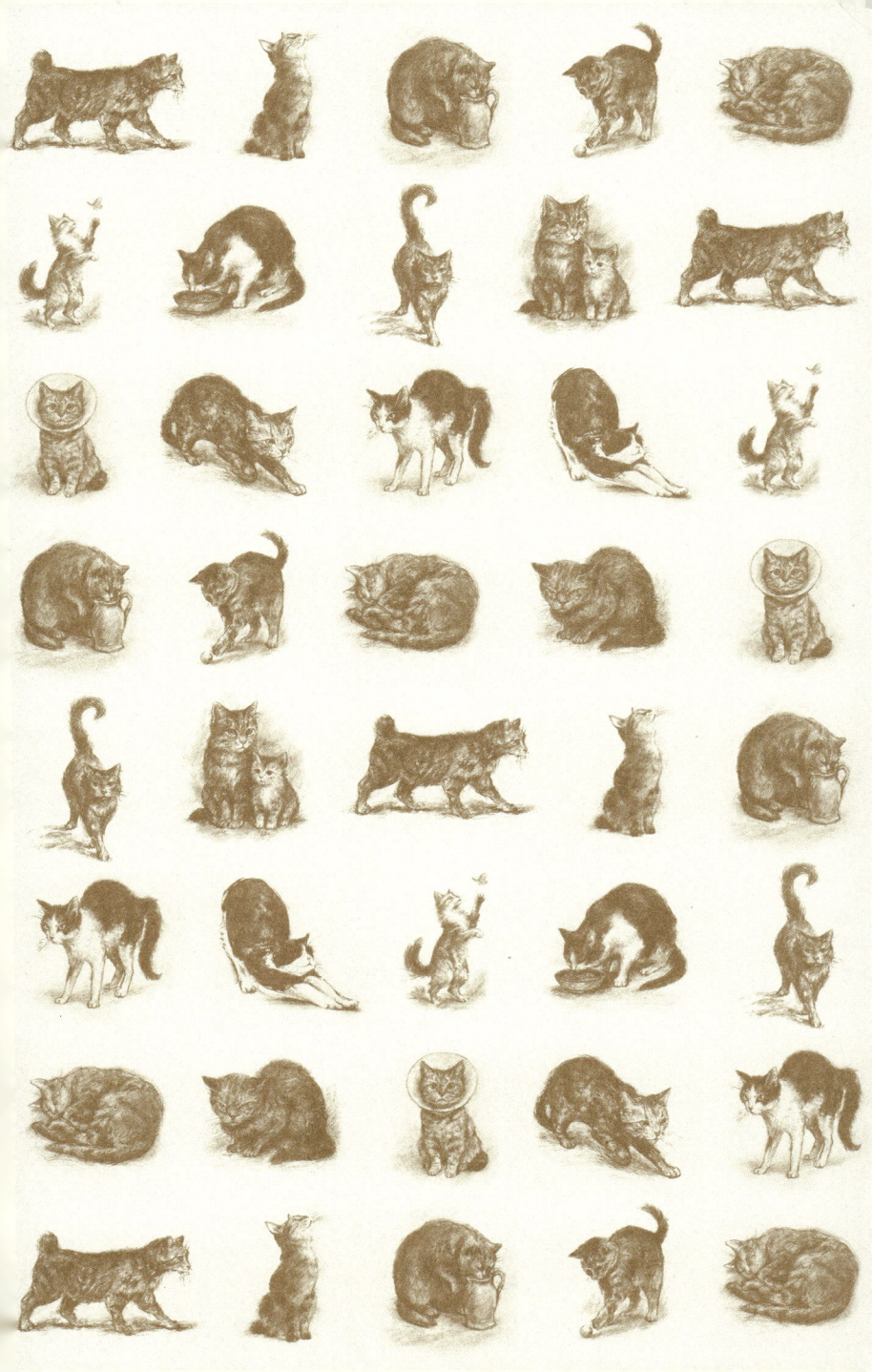

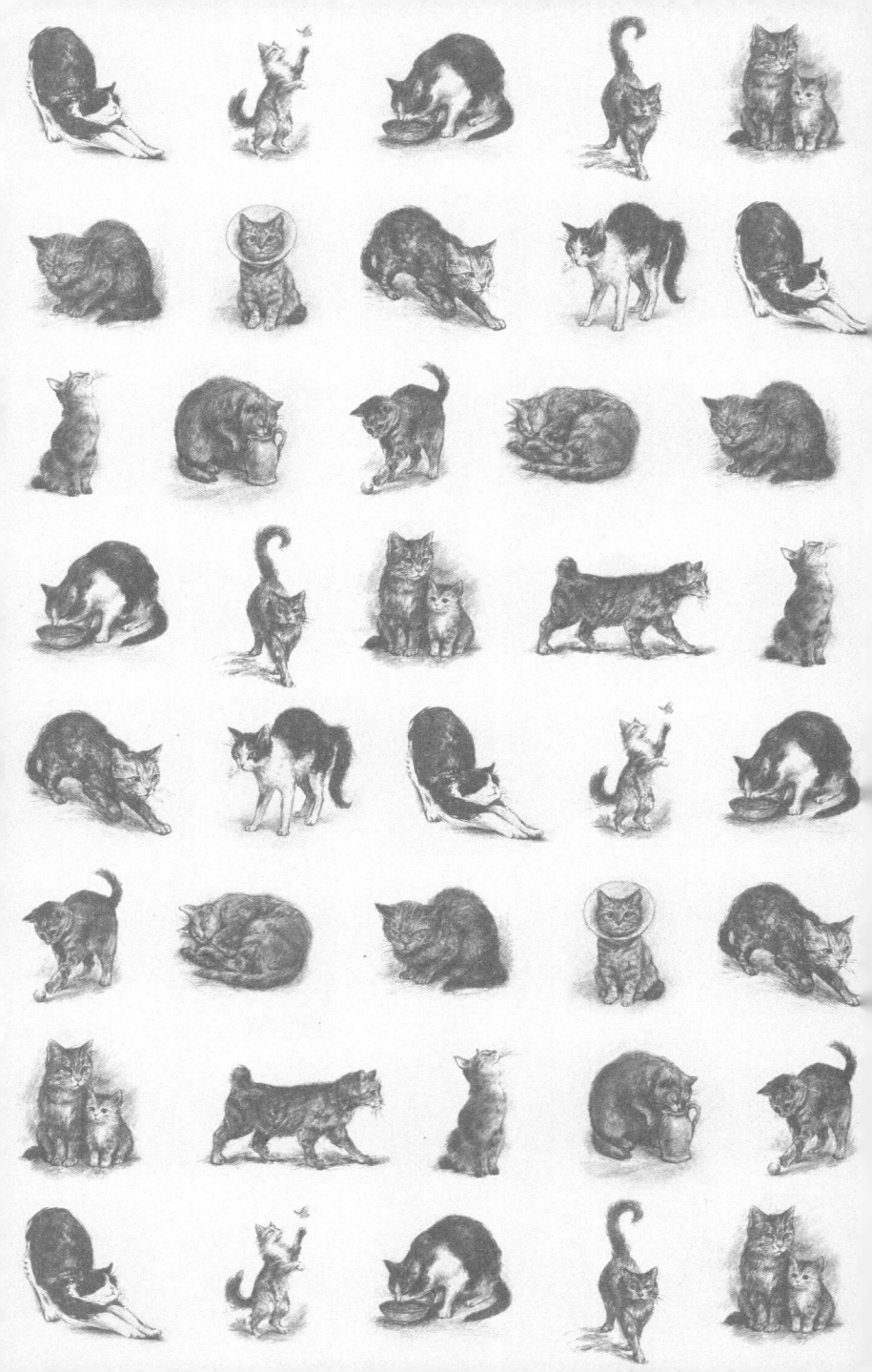